On the Banks of Damodar

On the Banks of Damodar

(Translated from Marathi)

Mr Anant Joshi

Tanslated by

Mrs Jayashree Naidu

KALPAZ

ISBN: 978-93-5324-010-3

First Published, 2019

Published by

Kalpaz Publications
C-30, Satyawati Nagar,
Delhi – 110052
Ph.: 011-47034999, 9811692060
www.kalpazpublications.com
E-mail: kalpaz@hotmail.com

Printed at: G. Print Process, Delhi

Disclaimer

This is a work of fiction. Names, Characters, incidents, name of places or cities used, institutions or industries are either the products of authors imagination or used fictitiously and any resemblance to any actual living person or dead, events or locales and institutions is entirely coincidental.

Anant Joshi
E-mail: pamsnehal@yahoo.co.in

Dedication

to the memory of

My eldest brother

Reverend Late

Sharad P. Joshi

Preface

My First book, Marathi poetry "Ek Avegala Mrityu" was published in the year 1996.My first Hindi novel "Geeta Chali Gai" has been published in 2013.My second novel "Beg your pardon" has been originally published in Marathi in 2015.This has been translated in Hindi and English and published in 2015.The Bangala version is under publishing.

Now my fourth book "On the banks of Damodar" is being presented to readers. This book is originally written in Marathi by name "Damodarachya Tirawar" and published by Vijay Prakashan, Nagpur. The Hindi translation is underway.

I do not know, whether any author has previously written on impersonation of workers .I found this subject different and interesting, which is called Banihari in local parlance and this practice is exploiting the poor people. So I decided to write on it. This corruption aspect is a serious socio-economical problem. The readers will gauze whether the problem has been depicted effectively or not. Another social aspect raised in this novel is "When a man can KEEP a woman, what is wrong if a woman has KEPT a man ?"

I am indebted to so many of my relatives and friends who have encouraged me for writing the novels. This encouragement fills new energy to write more novels.

I am thankful to Mrs. Jayashree Naidu from Solapur, Maharashtra, who has done excellent translation.

I am thankful to the team at Kalpaz Publications for facilitating the publishing of this novel in short span of time.

I pray to God, that readers should find the book interesting.

Thanks to all.

On the Banks of Damodar

Kirti Patel glanced at the date as she straightened up the folding calendar on her desk, 5th July 2000. She had been away on a week-long vacation to Kolkata and had resumed her duty today. A group of trade union leaders were already in her office pestering her to look into workers' issues. As a Senior Labour Welfare Officer, she had to handle labour union matters and over the years she had got quite accustomed to it.

"I'm sorry, I was away so you had to go through all this trouble," she smiled at them reassuringly, "I will certainly look into your applications." With practiced efficiency she quickly ruffled through the sheaves of papers that had been stacked on her desk during the week. She checked if there was a meeting or an appointment scheduled for that date. There was none.

The telephone rang. "Hello", she answered.

"Hello Madam".

"Hello", she said recognizing the voice at the other end.

"Hello, Madam, I am Ashok Kumar speaking. There is a problem here, you need to come urgently."

That call was from coal loading point at railway siding by Mr. Ashokkumar loading supervisor.

"What exactly has happened?" She asked.

"The Vigilance team has arrived. Please get Ramnaresh Yadav along with you."

Expressing her need to leave immediately, Kirti stood up and apologized to the labour leaders with folded hands.

Kirti headed straight for her jeep. She instructed the driver to drive her to Ramnaresh's house. The driver steered speedily along the road that lay by the banks of the river Damodar. The breeze that came blowing over the magnificent expanse of the river felt cool against her fair and beautiful face. She straightened the loose strands of hair that brushed against her face. On seeing the jeep pull up, Kamini, Ramnaresh's wife came out hurriedly and with folded hands informed Kirti that Ramnaresh had just left on his motorcycle for the site.

Kirti asked the driver to turn the jeep back towards the coal loading point. There were a few railway wagons parked at the railway siding near the coal loading point. The task of loading the coal into the wagons had come to a halt. Ramnaresh Yadav spotted her jeep arriving and greeted her with folded hands.

"How many people have been caught?" She asked.

"Three people", he replied.

"Just three of them?"

"All the Baniharees (impersonators) took to their heels. Only mine, Janu Prasad's and Ayodhya Prasad's did not run away."

"Let me see what I can do", she said.

She saw the Vigilance team standing in front of the Loading Supervisor, Ashok Kumar's office. Mine Manager Prabhunath Singh and Sales Manager Deepak Chatterjee were with the team.

"You are late, Madam", said Prabhunath Singh reproachfully.

"I wasn't told about it earlier." She said.

"Yes, we also got the information late," He said.

"Can we do something about it now? Will these people accept any explanation? Ramnaresh is pleading for help." Kirti asked with concern.

Prabhunath Singh replied, "Even Janu Prasad fell at my feet asking for some help, but Ayodhya Prasad hasn't approached us so far."

"Let's see if we can figure out something. I will ask Ramnaresh to arrange for some cash; perhaps he has already brought some," said Kirti.

The manager said he would talk to Ramesh Varma, the Vigilance Officer and try to convince him.

Kirti urged him to try his best to have the matter resolved.

Manager Prabhunath Singh and Deepak Chatterjee went over to Ramesh Varma. They took him along to Ashok Kumar's office for a discussion. Ramesh Varma called in other members of vigilance team. On conclusion of the discussion, Prabhunath Singh met Kirti and sent for Ramnaresh and Janu Prasad.

"Mr. Varma is asking for a bribe of Rupees 25,000/-each for settling the case of three Baniharees, (impersonators) a total of Rupees 75,000/-" Prabhunath Singh said

"That is a lot of money," Kirti remarked.

"Try to clinch the deal for a total of 50,000/- rupees, Sir. I have brought 15,000/-rupees and Janu Prasad has 10,000/- on him. Tell him we will pay up half the amount now and send the rest later. I shall pay up for Ayodhya Prasad's share at the moment and recover from him later. He has presently run away to his native village in Buxar district," offered Ramnaresh.

Prabhunath Singh said, "I don't think the officers will agree to this."

Kirti doubted, "What if they don't?"

"In that case we will have to invite them over to our Guest House and please them with good liquor and hold them there till we arrange for the entire amount of rupees 75000", said Prabhunath Singh.

Ramnaresh said, "Sir, try to convince them. These vigilance officers come here often and settle for Rupees 15,000/-per Baniharee (impersonator). Why are they demanding rupees 25,000/- for each now?"

Kirti requested Prabhunath Singh to try to speak to the officer once again and even offered to speak to them herself.

"No, no, you don't get embroiled in this murky matter. Deepak, Ashok Kumar and I will look into it." Said Prabhunath Singh

In fact such matters could not have happened without the covert permission of the manager and the loading supervisor.

Prabhunath Singh advised Ramnaresh to pay up Rs 25,000/- to Ashok Kumar, when he will hint him. He cautioned him to do it in the shadow of the jeep away from public sight.

Ramnaresh gave a nod in agreement.

Prabhunath Singh again held a closed-door meeting with Ramesh Varma in Ashok Kumar's office. He came out with Ashok Kumar. Then Ashok Kumar told Kirti who in turn gestured Ramnaresh to give the money to Ashok Kumar. The exchange was made secretly in the rear shadow of the jeep.

A little distance away, Jaggu Manjhi and two others were standing with Ramlal, their clothes covered in coal dust. Jaggu and two others had been caught by the vigilance team while loading the railway wagons with coal. Ramlal was a regular government loader.

Ashok Kumar handed over the money to vigilance officer Ramesh Varma with a promise to give the balance payment the following day. Ramesh Verma accepted the half-payment rather reluctantly.

Ashok Kumar ordered everyone to get back to their task of loading the coal. Everyone dispersed except Jaggu Manjhi and Kali Manjhi. Ramesh Varma, Prabhunath Singh and Deepak Chatterjee got into a jeep and headed towards the guest house. There was going to be an alcohol party there.

Kirti, Janu Prasad and Ramnaresh walked towards Jaggu and Kali Manjhi. Ramnaresh began to thrash Jaggu Manjhi and Janu Prasad beat up Kali Manjhi. Kirti pleaded with them to stop beating Jaggu Manjhi and Kali Manjhi, who were pleading guilty and begged for mercy. Finally, Ramnaresh stopped beating and asked why he had not fled the place at the arrival of the vigilance team when others had managed to escape.

Jaggu explained that they were loading the last of the wagons and had no idea what was happening in the front of the wagons. We heard someone calling us, so we came forward. They asked for our identity cards, and then we realized that we were trapped.

"Okay, get away from our sight now, "said Ashok Kumar. Jaggu and Kali disappeared into the distance.

Ramnaresh Yadav thanked Ashok Kumar. Kirti walked towards the jeep. Ramnaresh followed her and when she was seated in her jeep, he joined his hands, "Pranam, Madam," and lightly touched her feet in respect. Kirti smiled at his humility and left the scene.

This put an end to that day, but only temporarily, to a scandal that blotted the loading siding at the Maraal Coalmines. But it was just a temporary reprieve.

Ramgadh Coalfields Limited, RCL for short, was a public sector enterprise of government of India in Jharkhand state. The company had its headquarters at Ramgadh, a district place, 40 kms away from Ranchi, capital city of Jharkhand state. Ramgadh Military Cantonment is also located near Ramgadh city.

The coal mines were spread in an area about 200 kms around Ramgadh. All the mines were located in the vicinity of the Damodar river. Ramgadh Coalfields Ltd. Was divided into six administrative areas, looked after by General Manager each. Maraal mine was a part of Ichotu area.

Maraal mine was located on the banks of the Damodar river.

The coal belt actually stretched all along the Damodar river basin right up to West Bengal state.

The team of Vigilance Officers had come to Maraal all the way from Ramgadh Headquarters to investigate an 'Impersonation charge'. It was a common practice in the coalfields of Jharkhand and West Bengal for government workers to hire private labour in their place to work in the mines. These illegally hired workers were called 'Baniharee' in local jargon. The government workers were paid Rs.20,000 to Rs.24, 000 a month per month. The worker would sub-hire someone on a daily wage of a meager Rs 150–200 a day. The poverty-stricken people in that area had no choice but to accept these low wages for subsistence. While the government workers' salaries would be credited monthly into their bank accounts, the Baniharees (impersonators) were paid weekly wages. This was sheer exploitation of poor unemployed people in that part of India.

Ramnaresh Yadav and Janu Prasad were on the government roll and Jaggu Manjhi and Kali Manjhi were their impersonators or Baniharees. Ramprasad and Janu Prasad would never work on duty themselves; their Baniharees Jaggu and Kali did their work on the coal loading point at the Maraal coal mine.

Jaggu Manjhi returned to his hut in the afternoon. Radha, his wife worked as a maid in others' houses. She had not yet returned from work. He had his aluminum tiffin box with him. He felt the heat of the afternoon sun. He did not have an appetite either. But he opened his tiffin and finished the food in it. He then lay down his tired body on an old, soiled mat on the floor. He tossed and turned, his mind was in turmoil. He must have dozed off for about five minutes when the sound of Radha's footsteps woke him up. She was drinking a glass of water she had taken from the earthen pot.

She came and sat beside him. The look of helplessness in his eyes agitated her. "What is the matter?" She asked.

"There was another vigilance raid today." He told her.

Tears streamed down Jaggu's cheeks. She pulled his head towards her and gently wiped his tears with her pallav. "Did that bastard hit you again?"

Jaggu nodded and again wept in agony. She put his head on her lap and wiped his tears. This time she could not hold back her own tears. He put his hand to her eyes. She bent down and laid her cheek against his, both writhing in the hopelessness of their situation.

"Shall we give up everything here and go to our Kundapara in Birbhoom district?" He asked.

"What can I say?" She replied.

"I can't make up my mind too. I wish to go there. But it is difficult to find a job even in a district place like Birbhoom, let alone find one in the small village of Kundapara." Jaggu said.

She was quiet. He said they would talk about it later.

Both lay quiet. She adjusted the old curtain at the door and lay down beside him. They rested their hands on each other finding mutual comfort. He said, "You have to work really hard, don't you?"

She said, "I am accustomed to it. Life has never been easy since childhood. Nothing is different now. This is our destiny."

He gave a deep sigh, "Yes, true, this is our destiny."

"It is our fate that we are treated as animals, not as human beings." Radha said.

He fell silent for a while and the said, "You are right. Aren't we human beings?" (Aami ki Manus nai – in their mother tongue Bengali language)

He was pondering over his fate as a poor man. His poverty had made him vunerable to be treated below the normal human being. He felt that this poverty is attached to him like the skin of the body.

They lay quiet for some time. Then Radha got up. She took some raw rice from a box and stood at the door drawing apart the curtain. She began to pick the rice. Fortunately; she had fetched water in the morning saving her a trip in the afternoon.

In the evening Jaggu went to Ramlal's house, in the tiny miners' quarters. He called out Ramlal's name. Ramlal came out and both had a cup at the shanty tea-stall by the roadside. Jaggu blurted out his woes to Ramlal. Ramlal tried to console him. Jaggu asked him whether he should continue his miserable life at Maraal or go back to Birbhoom.

Ramlal said," What can I say; it is for you to decide. But don't take the decision in a hurry. First go back to work tomorrow. Ashok Kumar will not be able to stop you because Ramnaresh pays him. Let few days pass, and then you can decide."

Jaggu remained quiet.

Ramlal also worked as a coal loader on the wagons. But he was a government worker. He had been working in the mines much before the coal mines were nationalized. After nationalization, both he and his wife were regularized into government service. Now Ramlal's wife was no longer in service. His daughter-in-law Parbati had been given a job in place of her deceased husband. She worked as a peon in the mine office.

Jaggu finished his ablutions the next morning. Radha made him breakfast and wrapped his lunch box in a piece of cloth. Jaggu set out for work. Ramnaresh was already there at the site. Ashok Kumar, the loading supervisor asked him to report for work. Kali was told to do the same. Ramnaresh gestured Jaggu to leave; "Jaggu, stay alert at work," Ramnaresh cautioned him. Jaggu nodded rather solemnly. Ramnaresh departed with Ashok Kumar's permission.

---

8 July 2000

There was a flurry of activity in the Commissioner's Office at Hazaribaug today. The trimester meeting of all the District and Tehsil level Revenue and Municipal Corporation officials was scheduled for today. The Police Commissioner had also been invited for the meeting. Therefore, all the Superintendents and Deputy Superintendents of Police had also been summoned for the meeting. There was a fleet of white Ambassador Cars and Government jeeps lined up outside the office.

Two officers had arrived from Ramgadh. One of them was the Deputy Collector Mr. Kripal Singh and the other was Deputy SP Miss Renuka Mane. First the revenue matters were discussed followed by an assessment of the various government schemes especially with reference to social aspects. Then the law and order situation was discussed. The Commissioner asked for a total check on the illegal transportation of coal. He made it clear that the order had come from the Home Ministry at Ranchi. He also ordered a control on illegal construction activities.

This resulted in a lot of controversial discussion. Several officers blamed the coal mafia for the increased presence in the mines. Coal was being transported illegally on the streets generating a lot of black money dealings. Coal was stolen at the mines because their senior officials had no control over the activities at the coal mines.

Renuka Mane declared in no uncertain words that senior officers at the coal mines were involved in the illegal mining and transportation of coal.

The police commissioner objected to this allegation. He remarked that unless they had irrefutable evidence, it was not right to make such an allegation.

Renuka asserted that without the connivance of the officers, such illegal activities were impossible to carry out. The Deputy Collector Mr. Kripal Singh opined that RCL was a central government undertaking and the state government had no jurisdiction over it.

Renuka declared that the illegal selling of coal was generating a lot of unaccounted money which gave the mafia the money power to start illegal construction activities.

Kripal Singh strongly objected to this observation.

Renuka promptly asked him why he was not putting a check on the illegal constructions.

Her comment irked Kripal Singh. He became belligerent. The Commissioner pacified them. He observed that each one of them needs do his/her work diligently and curb any illegal activity they came across within the sphere of their authority.

The Deputy SP of Rajarappa mentioned that there was an unnecessary interference and involvement of politicians in our affairs.

The Commissioner offered to take due cognizance of such political interference if it was brought to his notice and also take up the matter with the Ministry if required.

The meeting was followed by a lunch break in which the attendees were provided packed lunches. The menu included poori-bhaji, one samosa and a large piece of kalajamun.

The scheduled lunch break for 20 minutes extended to 30 minutes quite naturally.

After lunch was the presentation of statistical data. All District and Tehsile level data ranging from revenue collection to crime rates was projected on a screen. Officers of the Municipal Council, of the Tehsil and District were able to make a comparative analysis of the figures. Print outs of these data were given to each one of them.

The Municipal Chief of Jhumritalayya requested the Commissioner to incorporate 8–10 villages around the city into Jhumritalaiyya because of the growing urbanization of these villages in the wake of new residential constructions and schools.

The Commissioner wanted to know the reason. The municipal -chief replied that it would generate more revenue to carry out the official development programmes in planned manner.

The Commissioner instructed him to send a proposal through the Collector and he would then look into it.

The Commissioner in a lighter tone, commented that Jhumritalaiyya was now featured on Google maps, earlier it was on All India Radio. This brought a smile to everyone's faces.

The meeting concluded. Renuka was curt when Kripal Singh tried to greet her. Kripal Singh smiled to himself. He shook hands with the other male officers and bade them goodbye. Each one went his way. Renuka felt that in this male dominated buracracy, being a woman is like outcast.

Renuka called on the Gokhale family residing in Hazaribaug. Mr.and Mrs. Gokhale were both Professors at the Hazaribaug University. Mr. Gokhale taught Sanskrit and Mrs. Gokhale taught Hindi. Both had Doctoral degrees in their respective subject. Mrs. Gokhale was at home when Renuka visited them. She made some tea and just as Renuka begged her leave after partaking of the tea and biscuits, then Mr. Gokhale returned home. They again reminisced about Satara, their place. The Gokhales urged her to have dinner, but Renuka declined. She returned to Ramgadh in the evening.

Renuka was back at her routine the next morning. She visited three-four police stations. Every where she noticed it was the same type of cases—thefts and fights. She then made a round of the bus terminal. The moment the auto rickshaw drivers spotted her jeep, they began to flee. An auto rickshaw was parked right in the bus stand. The driver felt the police baton on his back and quickly apologized, "I have made a mistake madam, wrong parking," before driving away his rickshaw from the scene.

It was Renuka who had brought some discipline at the bus stand. She had strictly enforced the rule that autorickshaws should park at the autorickshaw parking lot only and not obstruct the passage of buses within the terminal. She had managed to curb to some extent the practice of overloading jeeps and trax vehicles with passengers. She had allotted spaces for parking jeeps and matadors in a proper queue outside the terminal.

Prior to Renuka taking up office there, all these vehicles would crowd into the bus stand. The bus drivers were harassed and irritated by this obstruction and sometimes there would be minor accidents. Renuka had used her police stick liberally to beat up erring vehicle drivers and disciplined them. Earlier, there would be such bottle necks that even trucks had to maneuver through narrow spaces. Renuka had managed to ease the traffic jams to quite some extent that facilitated ease of traffic. She had also reduced the incidents of thefts; increased patrolling at nights and closed down gambling dens.

She had started a continuous correspondence with the Deputy Collector and Municipal Council Office to have the streets cleared of encroachment done by wayside hotels and eateries. The Municipal Council officers used to turn a blind eye to this encroachment. But on receiving strict instructions from the Deputy Collector, they would take action. Renuka Mane had earned the sobriquet 'Jhansiwali' in that part of Jharkhand for her tough implementation of law and order. No one had dared to work so fearlessly before. Criminals feared her tough approach. At first the inspectors and constables under her command did not cooperate her. After she suspended a couple of constables for dereliction of duty, everyone fell in line. Although they hated her for stopping their 'under the table income' but were too afraid to express these feeling and pretended to be happy working under her.

Renuka had an imposing personality. She was 5'6" tall. She had a wheatish complexion, sharp features and was smart looking. She had an eagle nose. She had cut her once long hair and now plaited a small braid. She had a well-toned exercised body.

She had been a captain of the Khokho and Kabbadi (Indian games) teams while studying at her school in Vita, District Satara in Maharashtra state. Her father was an ex-serviceman, retired from the army. He was full of patriotic fervor and constantly engaged in the service of the nation and the public. Renuka had reached this enviable status in life due to her father's motivation.

Her altercations with Kripal Singh were not new. They had differences of opinion on many issues. Kripal Singh was tall and podgy, with a somewhat long neck, a squarish face, small ears and close-cut hair. He was outspoken. His father was the Tehsildar of Devariya in state of Uttar Pradesh state. They also had some agricultural land in the district. As a result of his position as Deputy Collector, Kripal Singh wielded considerable power. Politicians of Ramgadh hobnobbed with Kripal Singh. His predecessor would get frequent dinner invitations from politicians. In recent times, although not totally stopped accepting these invitations, but Kripal Singh made them less frequent.

One afternoon, on the fifth day after the meeting at the Hazaribaug Office, Renuka took a stroll down the road leading to Maraal. This road lay to the left of the road leading to Ranchi. It ran along the bridge built over the Damodar river. On the bridge, she spotted a tricycle rickshaw filled with coal. It looked overloaded. The rickshaw puller was drenched in sweat. She stopped him. He was overcome with fear.

"Whose coal is this?" She asked him

"Mine." He told.

"Have you stolen it?" She asked

"No, madam, I have not stolen it. It is the coal that falls out of the coal trucks as they pass along. I have collected this fallen coal. Part of it belongs to two of my neighbors too. This month we were able to collect in excess so..." He told somewhat confidently.

"What do you mean, excess?" She asked

"We use it as fuel in our coal stoves; this is what was left after use." He told

"Who are you going to sell it to?" She asked.

"Sethji" He told

"Which Sethji ?" She asked

"Madan Seth." He replied.

"You mean Madan Oza?" She asked

"Yes, Madam sahiba." He said

"Let's go to him. You go ahead and make your sale. We'll follow you." She ordered him.

"Please don't ask me to do this, madam. That Seth will afterwards send his goons after me and have my legs broken." He pleaded.

"I see. Well then, let's go to the police station. I will break your legs there." She said

"Okay, take me to the police station, not to the Seth. I am a poor man, madam." He uttered.

Renuka found out that the man's name was Baldev. He lived in Maraal. She felt sympathetic towards the poor man and asked him to take his cycle rickshaw and wait at the police station near the bus-stand.

He obeyed.

She warned him not to give her the slip and run away. She had to attend to some task at the moment.

He shook his head in the negative, indicating he will not flee away.

When she reached the police station after an hour and half, she noticed that he had piled up the coal by the wall nearby.

She asked the constable if an entry had been made in the register. He said it had been made.

The constable told her that the man, Baldev had begged to be allowed to make a phone call. He had called up some officer at the RCL to get a bail for him.

Renuka said it was okay and asked the constable to hold Baldev at the station itself while she herself went home for her lunch. When she came back from lunch, she noticed an RCL jeep parked in the premises of the police station. On approaching, she saw a fair, beautiful woman in her 40's, sitting in the verhanda of office. The lady was dressed in a blue silk saree, had a chiseled face and a good figure. She had a string of pearls round her neck. She got off the jeep and greeted Renuka politely, "Good afternoon, Ma'am."

"May I know your name please?" Renuka asked.

"I am Kirti Patel, senior Labour welfare Officer at Maraal Coalmine" She said

"Oh, I see. And what has brought you here?" Renuka pretended ignorance about Baldev's matter.

"I have come to make a plea for Baldev's bail." Kirti told.

"Are you aware of the nature of his offence?" Renuka asked.

"Yes, madam." Kirti said

"Still you have come all the way from your office to make this request?" Renuka asked.

"That's because he lives in my house, I mean, he lives in the neighborhood." Kirti told.

"Well, this time I will release him in deference to the request made by such a senior officer like you. But please warn him that if I catch him transporting stolen coal again, I will show him no mercy." Renuka told politely.

"Yes, Ma'am, as you say." Kirti acknowledged. She thought that Renuka seems to be straight-forward.

There was a momentary silence. Renuka asked the sub-inspector to release Baldev.

Kirti said," I've heard a lot about you, but have met you in person only today." Kirti said.

"What did you hear, nothing terrifying, I hope?" Renuka enquired.

"No, only complimentary things—the common public sings your praises for improving Ramgadh, bringing crime under control and....." Kirti told

"And what?" Renuka asked.

"I have heard that some people are really afraid of you." Kirti said smilingly.

Renuka also smiled, "That is all part of the job."

Renuka and Kirti shook hands and ended the meeting with polite goodbyes and promises to meet each other again.

Baldev was waiting outside. Kirti wondered why he had not gone home. She was concerned that he might not have had anything to eat.

He said he was just about to leave. Kirti gave him a packet of food that she had brought for him and asked him to have it in his rickshaw. Then she told him not to ply his rickshaw for the rest of the evening, but rather go straight home to Maraal. She herself had to go back to her office. Baldev nodded affirmatively.

Renuka was observing all the communication between Baldev and Kirti from a distance. She felt there was something more to the relationship.

Ramlal, the coal loader, returned home that evening. He was feeling relieved that there was no vigilance raid recently. He himself was a government employee so he had nothing to fear, but he had a soft corner for Jaggu and was concerned about his welfare. Ramlal had his official photo identity card and could distance himself from any controversy. The other colleagues had brought in impersonators (Baniharees) from different states of India. Some of them belonged to Jharkhand state; some were from Orissa or Bengal state.

Some of the Government labourers who had engaged impersonators, used to work elsewhere during duty hours or even look after their farms in their hometowns. These colleagues tried to ask Ramlal to manage the money dealings with impersonators in their absence but Ramlal didn't pay any heed. He asked them to handle it themselves and not involve him in it. He did not want to get involved in these murky affairs.

Ramnaresh, Ayodhya Prasad and Janu Prasad were a trio- in-arms. Ayodhya Prasad used to operate from his hometown in Buxar District looking after agriculture fields. Ramnaresh and Janu Prasad would look after his affairs in Maraal.

Ramlal's family consisted of his wife Janaki, daughter-in-law Parbati, granddaughter Saraswati and grandson Manoj. Manoj was studying for his diploma in a polytechnic college in Ranchi. Ramlal's son Shivlal had passed away. After Shivlal's death, his wife Parbati had been given a job on compassionate grounds.

On stepping into the house, Ramlal saw Parbati's brother was at home on a visit. The brother touched his feet as a mark of respect. Ramlal freshened himself up and put on fresh clothes. His work clothes had been blackened with coal dust from his work as a coal loader. Once he was seated comfortably, Parbati's brother emerged from the inner room and sat in front of Ramlal. So did Janaki. Parbati also stood there, her head covered with her pallav.

"Madho has brought a marriage alliance for Saraswati,"said Janaki.

"That's good. What does the boy do for a living?" Asked Ramlal.

Madho told him that the groom is a supervisor with a builder. Earlier he had been a brick layer at a builder's. He earns Rs.10,000/ per month. He was presently working on big government building project. His parents and younger sister lived in village near Palamu.

The elder brother was married and lived in Lalitpur city in Madhya Pradesh state.

Ramlal asked whether the groom had any addiction. Madho said just the occasional liquor only that the tribals were used to drinking. That too only on Sundays, like everyone else.

Parbati added that the groom had been given a room in the same building that he was constructing. Since the construction would go on for two to three years, living quarters was not an immediate problem.

Ramlal was agreeable to the proposal. He suggested that a meeting with the groom's parents could be arranged at Hazaribaug, where they could take Saraswati along and work out the formalities.

The next day being Sunday, Parbati asked her brother to stay on and partake of the Sunday lunch before leaving.

A dish of goat meat was the Sunday lunch menu. Manoj had also come from Ranchi. Like his father, he too had opted for the Electrical engineering branch and was currently doing his First Year Diploma.

During lunch, the topic of the marriage proposal for Saraswati was discussed again. When Madho teased her, Saraswati became bashful. She had discontinued her studies after matriculation despite wanting to study further as the girls in the tribal community they belonged to, did not go in for higher studies as it was difficult to find an educated husband for them. Besides, there was no college in the Maraal coal mine. She would have to go to Ramgadh or Ranchi for college education and this was next to impossible.

As per custom, everyone, including the womenfolk in the family, had a peg or two of country liquor before having their lunch. This was a Sunday custom in all Adivasi (Tribal) households. Most of the week's earnings would be spent on this Sunday treat. Although Ramlal and Parbati earned a tidy salary working at the government coal mine, their expenses kept mounting.

Madho said that back home these Sunday liquor routine had become less frequent. Parbati said it made sense to do so. Madho said that when there were guests or visitors however, all customs would be followed as usual.

Janaki suggested that the custom be discontinued in their household too. Ramlal objected to this.

Janaki said that his health was deteriorating. He had frequent bouts of cough and the coal dust was affecting his health. "Isn't this true, Manoj?" She asked her grandson.

Manoj looked at his grandmother. He secretly agreed with her. He was of new generation, and was exposed to city life. He found this custom hateful but could not say so in the presence of elders. Manoj thought that this practice is keeping the family backward.

Madho appreciated the mutton dish. Janaki told him that it had been prepared by Saraswati. Saraswati coyly countered it saying it was cooked by grandma, and she had only lent a helping hand.

Everyone laughed indulgently.

Parbati suggested to Madho to take a little rest after lunch, but Madho declined saying if he stayed longer, it would get dark by the time he reached Hazribaug. He would rather start early.

Parbati packed some goodies for Madho. Manoj escorted Madho to the bus terminus. When Manoj returned Parbati asked him if Madho had found a seat on the bus. Manoj replied that the bus was running late so Madho had taken a trax (jeep) to Ramgadh from where he would take a bus to Hazaribaug.

Parbati thought he must have been in a real hurry not to have waited for a bus.

With her husband's death, Parbati's responsibilities had increased. Getting Saraswati married would reduce at least one of her burdens.

Two years ago she had got Lakshmi, her eldest daughter married to a crane operator working at the Chhutkakana Mines. Lakshmi already had a baby daughter now. Her parents-in-law would visit her often. Her mother-in-law had taken care of her during child birth and post –birth confinement. She had not sent Lakshmi to her mother's home. Parbati had visited them to see her new-born grandchild. Later on Lakshmi's husband had brought her here but he went back and Lakshmi was able to spend a few days with her mother.

Parbati thought about those days when she had just lost her husband. She had been extremely worried about how the family would cope with. Even though her father-in-law was a big support, she would worry about the future. With Saraswati's marriage, she would have to think only about Manoj. She felt that as a widow and mother of three children, she is bound with responsibility.

Today Satish Trivedi had a meeting scheduled with Madan Oza. Madan Oza was known as a coal mafia don in Ramgadh. He was into several businesses. He managed to get coal supplies to run the brick kilns running illegally, that he claimed to have all along the banks of the Damodar river. He managed to obtain coal permits for all those coal-based businesses and then provide the necessary coal to others by collecting it from the mines. Small industries had to totally rely on Madan for their supply of coal because it was too much of a nuisance for the small businessmen to make endless rounds to the Sales Office of RCL Coalmines and bribe the officials for good quality coal. They found it very convenient to let Madan Oza handle this for them. Many times if the coal permit was given for only a few tons, they could get it increased through Madan Oza's intervention. Madan Oza was familiar with all the officials, from the top to the bottom, at Ramgadh Coalfields Limited.

Madan had a personality that suited his kind of work. He had a big, fair, round, pleasant face, over a fat body; beady, shining, mysterious large eyes, that seemed to be assessing the person in front of him, a large nose, a vermillion vertical dab on his forehead. He had a gold chain round his neck and several rings on his fingers. He was always dressed in a dhoti and light-coloured kurta; sometimes he wore a Nehru jacket over his kurta. He had a well-built wrestler-kind of body. He owned two vehicles, one an open-to-the-sky jeep, which he loved to travel in. Recently he had purchased an SUV, an Innova car.

A fleet of Truck vehicles would collect coal from different mines. Most of this coal would be transported to North India, Uttar Pradesh, Punjab, Haryana and Bihar states. There were huge coal depots at Mughalsarai, near Benares (Varanasi) where Oza would supply his coal. Stealing of huge quantities of coal was rampant in coalmines. It was also quite common to loot coal wagons and throw out coal out of the trains and later collect this coal for selling in the black market. Coal thefts were rampant in the mines of Gola, Chhitarpur, and Chhutkakana.

There were several coal depots that bought this stolen coal but Madan Oza's Depot was the largest. Some unscrupulous managers of coalmines would manage to stash away a truckload once a week or once a month by showing lesser quantity of stock. This stolen coal would be disposed off in the illegal market with the help of Madan Oza. He had hired a team of bodyguards for his own safety and to safeguard his business. These bodyguards would be called 'Lathaith' (baton holders).

Today Madan Oza had invited Satish Trivedi, General Manager, Sales (coal), Ramgadh Coalfields Ltd. over to his farm house. Madan Oza had purchased a farm off the Rajarappa road. His farm house was located deep into his village farm. He had got an approach road made for his private use. For this, he had used his influence with Gram Panchayat of a nearby village and the offices of the Deputy Collector of Ramgadh. He had bought this farm house in the name of a villager. On rare occasions, Madan Oza used this farm house as a luxury retreat.

Today being Saturday, Satish Trivedi was a bit relaxed. He took his Honda City car and presented himself at the farm house at 7.30pm. Madan Oza was of course there to receive him.

"Pranam, Sir, Pranam (greetings),"said Oza obsequiously. Trivedi shook Oza's hands with a smile and hugged each other and proceeded into the house, hand in hand. There were three rooms, one leading into the other in a straight line. All three rooms were air-conditioned. The outer room led into another room which had a door resembling a cupboard. This door opened into a well-appointed, spacious bedroom with a sofa set and other furniture. The bedroom had a back door in case one had to make a quick, stealthy, exit.

Trivedi made himself comfortable on the sofa and Madan sat on the single seater sofa. Both smiled and shook hands once again.

Oza said that he was very delighted that Trivedi had accepted his invitation.

Trivedi said that Oza had been entreating him for several days now and it would be impolite not to accept. There had been a meeting some days ago after Diwali.

Madan glanced at Trivedi who was wearing a red colored Tee-shirt and a pair of blue jeans. He was reeking of perfume. Trivedi was 5 '4" in height. He had a fresh, fair face. He had thick hair cut fashionably. He was of medium build and looked active. His eyes were a bit small and impish. He seemed to be energetic and romantic always.

Madan offered him a glass of water from the jug kept on the teapoy. Trivedi had a sip. He noticed a bottle of Royal Challenge Whisky, soda and an ice bucket on a stool placed near the teapoy. "You seem to have made all arrangements..." Trivedi said.

"We knew you were coming, you deserve nothing less...." Madan said.

Trivedi put his hand in the pocket of his jeans and pulled out a packet. He handed it to Madan. There were three coal-permits in the packet.

"Oh, very nice of you to get the coal permits yourself." Madan said.

"You would have come to my office tomorrow, I saved you that trip." Trivedi told him and further added "You must send an acknowledgement of these permits to my office."

"Yes Sir, yes sir," said Oza. He extracted an envelope full of currency notes from a small, black hand bag and handed it to Trivedi. Trivedi stuffed the envelope in his pocket. He did not bother to count the notes and Ozha did not mention also. Trivedi knew how much it can be, depending on the tonnage of coal applied for.

Just then the butler brought a plate of paneer, different snacks like pakodas, onion pakodas and fried peanuts. That was the beginning of the booze party.

Madan poured himself small pegs but large ones for Trivedi. When Trivedi objected Madan obliged by taking larger pegs.

"Sir, you haven't been to Kolkata recently, have you?" Madan asked.

"No, I haven't." Trivedi replied.

"Never mind, Sir. If we cannot go to Kolkata, we can get Kolkata here." Madan said smilingly.

"What do you mean?" Trivedi asked with astonishment.

"Sir, we believe in providing you the best of services, so we have got two call girls from Kolkata."

Trivedi was amazed, "Wow, you are incredible!"

"Sir, you care so much for poor people like us,"Madan said in his oily manner.

Trivedi just smiled.

Then He asked after a moment, "What about Saurabh Pandey?"

"Who, the one from Dhanbad?" asked Madan.

"Yes." Trivedi said.

"Well, he doesn't visit our area often now. He only comes to collect some coal on his old permits," said Madan.

"You gave him a good thrashing, right?" Trivedi asked.

"I had to, Sir. He was growing too big for his boots." Madan said.

"He had called us to Dhanbad once." Trivedi told.

"I know. You enjoyed his hospitality on that occasion." Madan said.

"You see, we cannot afford to displease anyone, "said Trivedi. Though he said these words to satisfy Madan Ozha, He knew well that Madan dislikes any type of mingling with that squandrel Sourabh Pande and any favour to him.

Madan called out the attendant to get some fried mutton liver for the table.

Trivedi was delighted. "You take so much care of our taste buds, Ozaji."

"That's nothing. If not for you, who else deserves such attention?" Said Madan.

There were two more rounds of RC whisky. This was followed by dinner. There was mutton on the menu.

After dinner, Madan asked, "Sir, would you like to rest for the whole night, or just an hour or two?"

Trivedi said, "It's just an hour's business. I'll finish it and leave."

Madan handed him a packet of condoms from the cupboard. He pointed to the bedroom door and said that there were two callgirls out there, Trivedi could enjoy both if he so wished.

Trivedi said one was enough.

"Pick your choice and send the other one out."

Trivedi said, "Sure, as you say. You can have the other girl. By the way, I will be on my way when I finish. I don't want to interrupt your pleasure."

There were two young girls in their mid-twenties in the room. Both were dressed in salwar-kurtas. Trivedi chose the one who looked fuller in build and sent the other one out. He bolted the door from inside.

Jaggu had come to meet Ramnaresh. Ramnaresh's musclemen had detained him at the door. He kept waiting for over an hour. Just as he was preparing to return, he was called inside.

Ramnaresh gave a wad of notes to Jaggu. Jaggu counted them and remarked that he was being underpaid considering the number of days he had worked.

Ramnaresh told him that because of his mistake, he had to pay extra money to Mr. Varma, so his wages for only two days had been deducted.

Jaggu muttered under his breath that this was unfair.

Ramnaresh abused him and warned him not to rave and rant or he would chop off his hands and legs. No more grumbling.

Jaggu left, feeling wretched and helpless.

While on his way back to his hut, Jaggu came across Ramlal who was on his way to get some groceries.

"Pranam Chachaji (uncle)," Jaggu greeted Ramlal.

Ramlal took Jaggu to a wayside tea-stall, called 'gumti' in local jargon.

They ordered two cups of tea. Ramlal looked at Jaggu's face, which seemed crestfallen. He asked with concern what the matter was and whether Ramnaresh had beaten him again.

"No, He didn't beat me." Said Jaggu

"Then why do you look so miserable?" Asked Ramlal.

"That bastard has cut two days' wages from my pay." Jaggu told.

"Why?" Asked Ramlal.

"He says he had to pay Mr. Varma some extra money," said Jaggu

"What does it have to do with your pay?'Said Ramlal.

"That is what is bothering me. I did not knowingly get myself caught; those vigilance people arrived all of a sudden that is why I got caught." Said Jaggu.

"This Ramnaresh is getting more and more brazen day by day. I have seen him in the past, when he went around in ragged clothes and worked with us." Said Ramlal.

Jaggu said "Now he has become a wealthy man with his buffalo business. He gets a salary of Rs. 20,000/- per month but baulks at giving me a measly Rs. 150/-per day. He provides good, wholesome milk to all the senior officers and dilutes the milk with water for all others."

"He even provides pure ghee free of cost to senior officers, ghee made from fresh cream!" Said Ramlal. He knew how the times have changed Ramnaresh because of his malpractices.

Tea was served and both sip their tea. Ramlal noticed that Jaggu has lost weight. He had been hefty and strong when he arrived. Thank God, he was not addicted to liquor; he only had it occasionally when someone urged him to. Jaggu wasn't fond of liquor at all. Inwardly, Ramlal praised Jaggu's control over his alcohol, otherwise he would have ended up like his son, dying early of alcohol addiction.

Jaggu noticed the sadness on Ramlal's face and asked him whether he was thinking about his deceased son, Shivlal.

Ramlal nodded his head in affirmation.

Jaggu told him to be strong and not to worry so much at his age; he already was burdened with other responsibilities.

He put his hand on Ramlal's shoulder to commiserate with him. Ramlal restored himself. Both had their tea and departed, each on his way.

Jaggu returned to his hut. Radha was still away at work. His meal has been cooked. But he didn't have the appetite for it now. His worries about making both ends meet with the little wages he has earned. He had not been able to repay the loan. His entire wages went into paying the interest. There had been a famine in Bengal state three years ago. His mother, on the command of his brothers, had sent him a letter asking for some money. He could not refuse his mother. At the time he had borrowed some money from a money lender and sent it home to his mother. There was never enough to repay the capital. He barely managed to pay the interest with a lot of difficulty. There would hardly be any money left for other expenses. He had never been able to indulge in anything for Radha. She loved fish so much. She could eat it every day if possible. But he felt miserable that he couldn't feed her fish often.

Jaggu longed to go back to Kundapara village in Birbhoom district, Bengal state. He regretted coming to Maraal. He had been enticed by Biplav Goap, a friend to come here. Biplav was not here any longer at Maraal, but Jaggu was stuck. His brothers did not want him back in Birbhoom and in Maraal he had to endure Ramnaresh's persecution. He wished he had not quarreled with his middle brother.

Jaggu suspected that his middle brother Keshu lusted for Radha. Keshu's wife Sonu always had a grouse with Radha. Here in Maraal, Jaggu was aware that many workers had a lascivious eye on Radha but were wary of Jaggu's strong and sturdy physique and would rather not provoke Jaggu and get bashed up by him. Besides, Radha was a decent woman, who walked with her eyes to the ground. Even if anyone teased her, she would ignore it and walk past. So, generally no one bothered her. Once, Jaggu had given a drunkard a good thrashing for teasing Radha. Since then everybody was rather afraid of Jaggu, except Ramnaresh.

Jaggu felt helpless in front of Ramnaresh only, as if Ramnaresh was his master, his God. It was because of Ramnaresh that Jaggu could get a few morsels into his stomach. Jaggu became meek and yielding in Ramnaresh's presence. Moreover, he could not think of alternate employment at other place, because of loan availed.

There would be no strength left in Jaggu after a thrashing from Ramnaresh. His two henchmen, Naval Prasad and Suresh Singh were cruel and terrifying. Ramnaresh had brought them from his village near Chhapra especially to wield terror among the Baniharees. (Impersonators) These two men, however, would put on the most submissive and servile demeanor when they distributed the milk. They would be a picture of humility, with a red gamchha (towel) wrapped over their head or shoulder, stooping their shoulders, addressing people as "Sir/Uncle, Brother-in-law/Sister/Mother/or Aunt," with hands folded in a servile manner.

Jaggu could not figure out why he had to suffer such a wretched, helpless existence. Back in his village Kundapara, he could work with so much dignity on his farm. Here he hated this slavish, suppressed way of life. Besides, he was worried about Radha. Ramnaresh had once said that Radha can work as maid in his house but Jaggu had refused on the pretext that she was already overworked working as maid in several houses. Getting out of this miserable existence was Jaggu's prime concern and worry. His miserable life use to haunt him and make him more depressed.

To top it all, Radha always felt sad that she had not borne a child. Often he wished to take her to a good doctor in Ranchi or Ramgadh, but never had enough money to do it. The Government Hospital in Maraal took care of only government employees. Once in a while, some doctor would attend to them if they brought a reference from Kirti Madam, but he would be rather casual about it. Jaggu realized the need for Radha to get proper medical advice. She loved kids. She would find solace in playing with the neighboring children. She was very fond of Keshu's daughters but Keshu's wife Sonu would taunt her for being 'barren' and instigate her mother-in-law against Radha.

Tears welled up in Jaggu's eyes as he remembered Radha's words, "I am used to hard work, from my childhood I have had a hard life. This is my destiny." He wiped his tears and lay on the mat listless and sad.

Two girls from a local school asked for an appointment with the Deputy Collector, Kripal Singh. They were told by his Personal Assistant to come the next day. But the girls insisted on meeting him today. So, they were let into his chamber.

The two girls stood in front of Kripal Singh. Two people were already having a discussion with him in his office. The girls greeted him, "Pranam. Sir (greetings)"

Kripal Singh asked them what their purpose was. One of the girls stepped forward and handed a letter to him. Kripal read it.

"Where is this Vidyaniketan Junior College located?" He asked.

"In the Marwari Suburb, Sir." One of the girl told.

"Didn't your Principal think of someone else for this?" Asked Kripalsingh.

"Sir, DSP Mane Madam will be giving away the prizes." Came the reply.

"Then why do you need me?" Kripal Singh asked.

"We want you to be the Chairman, Sir."

Kripal thought over it for a moment. He sent for his P. A. to check if he had any meeting on Saturday, whether he would be free on Saturday afternoon.

The P. A. said he had no commitment for Saturday afternoon.

Kripal Singh said to the girls," Well, I will try to attend the event but on the condition that if anything else comes up I would not be able to keep my word."

"Okay, Sir."

"You may go now." He said.

The girls lingered on. "What is it now?" Kripal Singh asked.

"Sir, could you please write a formal acceptance letter to our Principal so that we can print your name on our Invitation Card?" Girl said.

"Write the acceptance on the Principal's letter itself. Keep a Xerox copy of it in your file and remind me of this event one day prior and on that day as well," Kripal Singh instructed his P. A.

As the girls turned to leave, he stopped them and said," On the day of the event, call my P. A.to remind him. You can take his mobile number from him."

The girls thanked him politely and left.

Madan Oza who was seated across the table all this while asked, "So you are going to be there along with Mane Madam...?"

"Well, one has to attend cultural and social events and mingle with the public." Said Kripal Singh, smilingly.

They laughed at this remark.

On Saturday, Renuka Mane reached the venue on time. She was attired in a light pink cotton saree instead of her police uniform. There was no sign of Kripal Singh. Renuka chose to sit in a chair in front of the stage rather than on the dais. A huge tent had been put up on the Junior Girls 'College grounds and it was already full with the students and parents.

She asked whether anybody had telephoned the Deputy Collector or not.

The Principal informed her that two girls had already left to escort him back.

Kripal Singh arrived shortly. He greeted Renuka with a Namaskar. Renuka returned the greeting with hands joined in a pranam.

The Principal lead both of them to the dais. The ceremony started with a prayer to Goddess Saraswati and lighting of the ceremonial lamp. The guests were then felicitated with garlands and bouquets. Formal introductions were made. The Vice-Principal gave a long winding foreword and a report of the academic and cultural activities of the college. Kripal Singh was feeling restless. The prizes for academic achievements were given away by Renuka. Fortunately, the speech by the Principal was short. Kripal Singh stole an opportunity to whisper to Renuka that in response to her request,a notice about encroachment had been served to the hotel near the station. The railway administration had also been informed because half the property belonged to the Railways.

Renuka thanked him and he smiled at her, feeling relaxed.

The next part was the distribution of prizes for achievement in Sports and Cultural activities. Most of the time, Renuka was asked to award the prizes but once in a while Kripal Singh was called upon to do the honors. Renuka was requested to give a speech. Renuka, in her speech, applauded the girls for their achievements and reminded them of the need to do something for society in future. She put in a word of praise for Deputy Collector

Kripal Singh too for the efficient administration of Ramgadh. She had to pretend that administration in general is one and in unison in front of these students.

Kripal Singh returned the compliment in his speech by praising Renuka for the decline in crime in Ramgadh and for making criminals fear the law. He mentioned that safety of women had improved. He emphasized that in order to achieve anything in life, one had to take inspiration from an ideal role model. Girls must look upon great women like Indira Gandhi, Kiran Bedi, Lata Mangeshkar and PT Usha as their role models. He looked at Renuka and said that there is a great woman among them now, who has come all the way from Maharashtra and improved the law and order situation. Someone who had made the streets safer for women. His words elicited a loud applause. Renuka blushed at first but collecting herself, she uttered a loud "Thank you" to him.

Kripal Singh and Renuka took their leave after the conclusion Vote of Thanks and the National Anthem. They discussed a new case about the coal mafia in Ramgadh. Kripal Singh assured her that she would have his full cooperation in this matter. Renuka is surprised but prefered not to comment. She complimented the Principal and her team for the programme and thanked them for inviting her. In return, The Principal thanked her for taking time to attend despite her busy schedule.

On her way back, Renuka pondered over Kripal Singh's behaviour. She wondered why an arrogant and pompous man like Kripal Singh had been so polite and full of praise for her. Perhaps he was building such an image of himself to impress the teachers and students. Renuka was aware that she would be sharing the stage with Kripal Singh because the Vice-Principal had said so when she had come to invite her. It had been both impossible and improper for Renuka to decline the invitation. She thought that had she not praised him, he would not have praised her back.

She remembered the initial antagonism of Kripal Singh towards her. When she had first demanded that an encroachment notice be served on the hotels near the station, he had passed it on to the

Municipal Council though the said land belonged to the Revenue Department.

It was very much in his official capacity to serve such a notice, but at that time he favored the hotel owners. Only when the order came from the Commissioner, the administrative machinery had taken action. Perhaps he had an inflated male ego. She knew that the coal transporters, the hoteliers and the coal mafia dared to defy her because they had Kripal Singh's support. But she had persevered and finally managed to cow them down. They now felt intimidated by her sternness and authority. She would arrest the criminals on Saturday night and present them in court only on Monday. She had the Court's support too. On the intervening Sunday, she would give the criminals a good beating with a cloth-wrapped stick. She ensured that there were no bruises or marks of the thrashing. She had established a good network of informers. She had picked up men who were poor and addicted to liquor and were ready to part with information for nothing more than a bottle of liquor. They were not greedy for more.

With these tips she could wield a strong control over the area of Ramgadh and nearby villages as well as the coalfields.

Then she thought that perhaps Kripal Singh had realized that his word carried no weight. Besides, the media was quite active. The law and order situation in Ramgadh would be discussed in Ranchi. Renuka had the tacit support of the Director General of Police. All these factors might have humbled Kripal Singh a little.

She had felt a little uncomfortable when Kripal Singh had looked at her approvingly during the function.

As she was dressed in a saree, she must have looked particularly appealing to him. She had not quite liked his discreet glances at her, but she wasn't upset either. There was no lust in his eyes; they were just appreciative glances of her physical attractiveness. She pondered over the incident, whether this is the first time or he had been eyening on her for quite a time. Being a bachelor, He must have habit of eve observeing.

The following day Renuka had got a call from Kirti. There was a labour unrest problem in Maraal and she wanted Renuka to send a police posse to Maraal. Renuka decided to go herself along with the force.

Maraal coalmine was divided into two portions: Maraal I and Maraal II. Maraal I was the underground section and Maraal II was an opencast mine.

It was a year and a half since Maraal II had become operational; yet it was only at the stage of digging up the earth. Coal was yet to be unearthed. This mine was probably going to be renamed.

Maraal I underground mine was located near the bank of the Damodar river. A part of it was under the riverbed so there was a chance of the mine getting submerged. There were huge pumps fitted into the mine to draw out water. That particular day, an accident had occurred in phase 4 of the mine. The coal wall had been drilled into. The holes had been filled with dynamite and exploded. The loose and broken coal blocks were being collected. Only the blasting foreman was present at the time of the blasting, the others had gone to the adjacent phase. A while later after the blast, the mining Overman and the Chief Miner (Sardar) had gone ahead. The Shift-in-charge Assistant Manager was yet to arrive.

The Chief miner (Sardar) had checked out the roof with a stick. A small portion in a corner of the roof had come off. He ignored it. Hardly had the task of collecting the coal into baskets started when a portion of the roof fell. Some mine workers were trapped under the broken roof. There was a commotion and cries for help. The rescue team had arrived. They were drilling the coal away. Some of the coal was being moved away with shovels. More number of rescue members were being called in to make the work faster. Work in the entire mine had come to a stop. Messages were being sent all over. The Safety Officer and the Security officer had arrived from Ichotu area office. Project Officer Santosh Kumar Sinha and Manager Prabhunath Singh had gone into the mine. Injured workers were being evacuated on stretchers and in lifts. Ambulances were on standby. Injured workers were put into the ambulances.

Kirti Patel tried her best to get their names and identity numbers or asked other workers to identify them. She was trying to ensure that there were no impersonators (Baniharees) or fake workers among the injured. As a welfare officer, she had to be viggilent on this account.

Towards the end of the rescue operation, two dead bodies were sent up in a lift. Prabhunath Singh was in the lift. He pretended as if the two workers were injured and tried to put them in an ambulance to be taken to the Mine Hospital.

But two workers in the ambulance screamed that they were dead bodies. The other workers were agitated. A riot ensued. Realizing the gravity of the situation, the Area Security Officer packed off the Project Officer Santosh Kumar Sinha and Manager Prabhunath Singh into a waiting jeep and drove it to the Manager's office.

By that time all work in all the phases of the mine had come to a standstill. The mob of all mine workers had begun to shout. One of their leaders instigated them to gherao the Manager. The atmosphere was getting charged with mob mentality.

Kirti was about to head to the hospital in her jeep. The moment she overheard the mob leader, she called up Renuka on the cell phone and asked for police protection. It took Renuka 45 minutes to reach the site. By then the workers had surrounded the Manager's office. The security officer and some guards were present there. The Mining Sardar and Overman had already been given a beating. Kirti took both of them to the hospital.

The mob of workers was abusing Sinha and Prabhunath Singh and were waiting to thrash them. Everyone was agitated and incensed. The area Security Officer was trying to pacify them with folded hands. But the workers refused to be calmed down and were becoming more aggressive by the minute. They were about to push the Security Officer away and enter the office. Inside the office, Sinha and Prabhunath were terrified and feared their lives. They were praying the God.

Renuka arrived at the scene with a van full of policemen. The mine workers were taken aback to see policemen arrive so fast. The sight of the policemen subdued the leaders a little. But they continued to shout in low tones, "Manager, come out!" Renuka started walking towards Manager's office. The workers started to give her way.

A couple of leaders would intercept her and say, "Madam, please arrest those two officers. They have caused the death of two of our fellow workers."

Renuka assured them that she would take the necessary steps as per the law.

By then the Government Safety Department team arrived to inspect the site. The team members entered the mine directly along with the area Safety Officer.

Prabhunath Singh and Santosh Kumar Sinha were relieved to see Renuka enter the office. "Thank you, Ma'am." They thanked her profusely for being there.

A labour leader shouted, "Come out, Prabhunath Singh." But there wasn't much strength in his voice. There were some policemen standing outside the office, some with rifles and some with sticks. The crowd of workers slowly dispersed. Some retreated from there. The labour leaders somehow managed to hold some workers together. The union leaders started realizing that their plan of violence has failed.

Other officers also arrived. There was a team from the Headquarters at Ramgadh. The Chief Personnel Manager of the area called four labour leaders into the office. Negotiations began. The leaders extracted a promise from the officials that the legal heirs of the dead workers would be given jobs. They were also to be given the money required to perform the cremation rites. The Chief Personnel Manager of the area came out and faced the crowd. The labour leaders impressed upon him to declare that the next-of –kin of the deceased workers would be given a job and also an amount of Rupees 10,000/- would be given to the families for the funeral rites. He also declared that the deceased workers' Gratuity would be paid within a week to the nominee heir. He also appealed to everyone to donate one day's salary to the deceased workers' heirs. He himself would contribute the same. He also avowed support of labour leaders. He announced the formation of a Committee to look into the workers' problems and collection of one day salary donation and nominated two leaders on the spot. He got their acceptance too. The leaders had no option but to say "Yes." The leaders had to save their faces, to sustain their shop of the leadership. The mob was pacified and began to disperse.

Santosh Kumar Sinha and Prabhunath Singh wanted to enter the mine as the Mine Safety Department was conducting an inspection. When Renuka said she wished to join them, the Personnel Manager of the area tried to dissuade her saying she might feel uncomfortable in the coal pit, but she insisted on going. She had never seen an underground mine before. After having a look at the exact spot, she came up to the surface along with the Area Security Officer. She had met the officials from government safety department and got information regarding procedure of fixing responsibility of accident After coming out, She brushed off the coal dust from her clothes and washed her face in the Washroom attached to the Manager's office. From there, accompanied by the Security Officer, she paid a visit to the loading point. She inspected the points where coal was loaded into trucks and into railway wagons. She admonished the Safety Officer for the lack of cleanliness and safety there. She then checked whether the Loading Supervisor's office is equipped with a First-aid kit. Afterwards she visited the hospital. She asked the team of policemen to go back to Ramgadh.

At the hospital, she met Kirti. Kirti took Renuka to the Doctor's Room, where they had some tea and biscuits. Kirti expressed her gratitude to Renuka, "Thank you, Madam, Thank you."

Renuka told to Kirti "It seems that you have timely called me"

Kirti said "I had no option. Otherwise there would have been fight between our security man and workers. May be officials would also have beaten, but first of all, the security personal in small numbers would have had heavy injuries."

Renuka bade her goodbye and returned to Ramgadh.

Kirti Patel was taking a stroll on the streets of Ramgadh on Sunday afternoon. She wanted to buy some clothes. There was a road leading from Barkakana village to Ranchi. There was a shopping mall at the corner of Ranchi Road. She entered the mall but found the clothes too expensive. Her next thought was to go to the market in the Marwari Suburb. She looked out for a cycle rickshaw to ply her there.

Renuka was passing by in her jeep. She saw Kirti standing on the road. "Good afternoon," Kirti was startled. She had not noticed when Renuka had come and stood behind her. Both shook hands with each other.

"Where are you going?" Renuka asked.

"Nowhere, just shopping for some clothes, night gowns and some such items." Said Kirti.

"Well, if you are not in a hurry, shall we have a cup of coffee somewhere?" Renuka invited.

"Sure, why not? My shopping isn't all that urgent." Kirti affirmed.

"Good. Then let's go over to my bungalow. We can talk at leisure." Said Renuka.

"Suits me fine." Said Kirti.

Renuka and Kirti arrived at the bungalow in Renuka's jeep.

Renuka took Kirti to her kitchen. There was a set of a small dining table and two chairs in the kitchen. Renuka offered a seat to Kirti. She then asked her maid to run the clothes washer and set about making the coffee herself.

She fetched the milk from the refrigerator and placed it on the table. Then she got some snack containers and plates and served biscuits and savories. She asked Kirti to have them while she placed the milk pot on the hob.

Kirti had a spoonful of the mixture and asked Renuka to have some too.

Kirti began to discuss the accident that had occurred at the mine. She told Renuka that the mine officers would have been in deep trouble if Renuka had not arrived in time.

Renuka was modest in her reply. She said, "It is our duty to maintain law and order. But I have noticed that safety measures are not strictly implemented at the mine. There ought to be very stringent safety measures. How is it that no one cares about the lives of the poor workers?"

"This is not exactly the fact, but sometimes we do falter."

By then the milk was heated. Renuka poured it into two mugs; then she added sugar and coffee powder and stirred it. She offered a mug of coffee to Kirti and seating herself on a chair, she had some coffee too.

"I have heard that you have impersonators working in the mines?" Renuka asked.

"Yes." Said Kirti.

"Where is the need for that? Why don't you stop this practice?" Said Renuka.

Kirti began to explain, "There are a few reasons for this. Way back before coal mines were nationalized, there was the practice of having substitute workers (Badali Mazdoor) to work in place of a worker going on leave or to work on his farm in the village. He used to keep a man to work in his place. This ensured continuous production of coal. It would save the management the trouble of getting new workers. At that time the real name of the substitute worker would be noted, because most of the hiring was recorded as casual labour in the muster. Only if there was to be some deduction from the provident fund of the original employee, then his name would be entered in brackets against the casual worker's name.

After nationalization, this practice of substitute labour was discontinued for a few days.

Very soon however, this became the basis for corruption. These substitute casual workers became Baniharees (impersonators). Earlier, two or three casual workers did the work of one official labourer. Nowadays, there is only one and he works for prolonged periods at a time. Instead of temporary work for ten or twenty days, they became permanent Baniharees. Officials at all levels of the administration became a part of this corruption network. It became a lucrative business. There is a lot of poverty here in Jharkhand and in Orissa and Bengal as well. The tribals in these areas are so poor that even two meals a day is hard to come by. There is rampant malnutrition. This evil of Baniharee system is a product of all these factors."

"Please don't mind my asking you, but do you also have a finger in this pie?" Asked Renuka hesitantly.

"No,not at all. I am not a part of this evil network. I don't take a single paisa. That is why the leaders and supervisors are in dread of me." Kirti informed.

"Doesn't your Headquarters try to put a rein on this?" Asked Renuka.

"They are trying but not enough. Probably some of the moolah (money) reaches Headquarters too. There are other types of Impersonators (Baniharees) like Weigh-bridge clerks who collect Rs 20 per truck load illegally. These clerks have appointed literate Baniharees, two to a post, each on a salary of Rs 10,000/- per month. These literate Baniharees oversee the parking of trucks at the weigh-bridge, weigh the quantity of coal,and make documents. The original clerk spends his entire salary on these Baniharees. But if they pass 150 trucks per day, his daily illegal earning amounts to Rs 3000/-. So his monthly illegal earnings amount to Rs 70 or 80 thousand. Probably this money reaches some people at Headquarters. I pity the poor illiterate workers, who come from far-off areas, live in slums, work ten to twelve hours a day loading coal into wagons; and at the end of the day they earn just 150 or 200 rupees per day. The main concern is value of human life."

Kirti and Renuka had finished their coffee by then.

Renuka remarked that they have had too much of 'Baniharee talk'.

"I agree," said Kirti.

"Let's change the topic."

"Fine." Said Kirti.

"Can I ask you about your marriage?" Asked Renūka.

"I am getting old now. I am unmarried and not likely to be married at all. Let's talk about you. You are still young, beautiful. We must talk of your marriage." Said Kirti.

"You are right. My family is looking out for a groom. But this police job, here in Jharkhand, far away from Maharashtra state poses a problem." Renuka told.

Kirti laughed and said, "Let me suggest something; don't be annoyed. Why don't you find someone suitable here in Jharkhand?"

Renuka brushed it off lightly.

"No, I really mean it. Pardon me for asking, but is there anyone courting you? It's just a casual question. Actually no one will dare to woo a woman police officer", Kirti said smilingly.

Renuka blushed at this remark. Kirti knew she had guessed right. "Tell me, do you have anyone in mind? You need not tell me the name."

" Nothing special that I can mention." Renuka hesitated.

"Nothing special, but something simple ?" Kirti remarked.

"In deference to your age, I must say you are not wrong in your conjecture. There is indeed one officer. In recent times, he has been trying to get close to me. But I feel he is a corrupt officer." Renuka told.

Kirti replied, "Forget the corruption. Carry on for a while. He will mend his ways in future. I won't ask you his name or his position. I must be taking your leave now."

"So early? We were having such a nice conversation. You haven't yet told me anything about yourself." Said Renuka.

"What is there to say about myself? Nothing interesting at all." Said Kirti.

"You are still beautiful. You must have been a great beauty in your youth. I am sure you must have been chased by many young suitors. They must have been besotted with you. Did you really not find anyone worthy?" Renuka casually said.

But Kirti became emotional. She looked grave. It was a different Kirti that Renuka was seeing. She too became grave.

"What is it?" Renuka asked. Kirti's eyes filled up with tears. She looked helplessly at Renuka.

"I am sorry," Renuka quickly got up and put a reassuring hand on Kirti's shoulder.

Kirti felt a lump in her throat. She wiped her tears. Renuka offered her a glass of water. Kirti took a few sips. She composed herself. Renuka came back to her seat.

Kirti avoided narrating her life story. She only told "I have very sad memories of Kolkata. So I came here to these jungles to be far away from Kolkata. Though I have tried to go away from Kolkata and the sad memories, I sometimes can not deny reimmergence of that grief in my heart. Some people are destined to be unhappy. There is a touching song by Mukesh: 'Yeh tere pyaar ka gam, ek bahaana tha sanam, apni kismet hi aisi thi, ki dil toot gaya. (Grief of your love, is just an excuse only. My destiny was as such that my heart broke)"

Renuka felt guilty about stoking Kirti's suppressed grief. Kirti may not like to talk about it in detail now. Who knows what pain, grief and despair lies buried in everyone's heart!. Renuka further thought that Kirti is like a beautiful painting drawn in dark colours full of shadows.

There was a silence for a while. Renuka told Kirti, "You can pour your heart out to me if you wish. But it is all right if you don't wish to talk."

Kirti remained quiet for a moment. Then she told Renuka that she would tell her complete life story some other time, at leisure. It was time to leave and for Renuka to attend office.

"How are you travelling to Maraal?" Renuka asked.

"I will take a bus or Trax (jeep) from the bus-stand. Or I may find the rickshaw driver of that day." Kirti told." That same rickshaw driver?" Renuka asked.

"Yes, the same one," Kirti says without hesitation.

"I will drop you at the bus-stop. Or is it alright if I ask my driver to drop you there?" Said Renuka.

"No problem at all."

Both came out to the front yard and Renuka instructed her driver to drive Kirti to the bus-stop in the jeep.

Kirti arrived at the bus-stop.

Baldev was waiting for her. He thought madam is looking a bit crestfallen. He asked her what the matter was.

She evaded a direct answer.

"You had come for shopping, haven't you made any purchases?" He asked.

"No. I haven't bought anything. Let's go." She said.

The cycle-rickshaw had by then left the main Ramgadh road and was on the road to Maraal. Realizing that Madam was in a despondent mood, Baldev made no further talk and speeded up towards Maraal.

Kirti got a jolt as the rickshaw went over a pot-hole on the street. She cautioned Baldev to slow down but he pushed on with speed. Kirti held on to a bar in the side of the rickshaw and said nothing to Baldev. Dusk had begun to set in. The sunlight had begun to fade. It was not yet dark. Kirti looked up at the sky. The birds were returning to their nests. The feeling of loneliness and emptiness defrezing, desolving her otherwise strong mind. The evening sky would make her distraught. The evening sometime made her woeful and secluded. Her subdued emotions would gush forth as reminiscences of her life in Kolkata would flash across her mind.

The lawns in front the Victoria Memorial at Kolkata looked lush green as usual, in day time. There were many couples enjoying a blissful togetherness. Most of these were young college-going boys and girls. There was one couple among them. Piyush Mandal and Kirti Patel were their names.

Both were studying for their final year Master of Social Work Course. (MSW).

Kirti was sitting at a modest distance from Piyush. He quickly moved close enough to touch her and put his arm round her waist. Kirti was wearing a pink kurta and reddish salwar and a pink, net dupatta.

"You are looking very beautiful today," Piyush said.

Kirti said coyly that she knew what was in his mind.

He smiled. She too gave a smile. She had an attractive smile.

"You are really looking so beautiful that I want to shower your face with kisses."

She gave a light pat on his cheek and said, "You are very cunning."

His hand began to caress her waist.

She said, "Wait, I have something serious to say."

"Say it. I love listening to serious talk." He pulled back his hand from her waist. He pulled up his legs close to his body and wound his hands around them tightly. "Come on, tell me."

"You see, my family has started looking out for an alliance for me."

"That's nice. Go ahead and look for a rich businessman from your community." He told mischievously.

"Don't make fun of me, please. I don't like it." Kirti said

"What should I do then?"

"Are you really going to marry me?" She asked

Piyush became grave for a while. Then he looked to the left and there pointing to a fat girl dressed in a green salwar, he said, "Look at her, I am going to marry her."

Kirti quickly got up and started punching his back in mock anger.

He began to laugh loudly. The other couples looked at them.

"Enough, you have punched me enough."

"Well, I must leave now." Kirti said.

"Wait, I'll drop you on my bike." Piyush said.

"No, I would rather take a bus."

"Come on; don't be so annoyed with me."

She relented and sat astride on his bike. She put her arms around his waist to hold him. As they reached near the turn at Hazra, he told her to hold him tighter.

"No, not on a thoroughfare like this."

"Just once," he begged of her.

She rested her neck on her shoulder. He inched back a little. She embraced him tightly. He felt her breasts press down on his back. Her hair blew against his face. He loved the sensation.

All of a sudden, the signal turned red at the Hajra square. They wanted to go left to Bhavanipur side. The car in front of their motorbike put on the brakes suddenly. Piyush too pressed the brake on his bike to avoid a collision. Kirti was jolted to her senses. When the bike took the left turn, she moved back a little and rested just one hand on his shoulder. She cautioned him to stop the bike just short of the Bhavanipur square, near Prasad Hotel. From there she intended to walk home.

"Let me drop you at your house."

"No. At this time, my boorish neighbors will be chatting with my mother in the apartment compound." Kirti said.

"Alright. As you wish."

Kirti wanted to walk home. She had to walk across the square, turn right and go to Lane number 3, where her apartment was located.

When she reached the apartment premises, two of her mother's boorish friends were already there. One of them said snidely, "College seems to have got over early today." The other one laughed.

Kirti climbed the stairs to her second floor flat in a huff.

Kirti's family comprised of her mother, two brothers and herself. Her father had died of a heart attack when she was still studying for her matriculation. He had worked as the Munim (treasurer) for a Gujrathi hardware merchant. This merchant had a flourishing cement supply business. Her father had left his native place, Jamnagar at the age of nineteen, in search of a livelihood. One of the merchant's relatives had brought him to the merchant in Kolkata. Despite having to borrow a loan, her father had managed to acquire a flat in Kolkata, which was his chief asset. The merchant, Thakur Bhai had helped him with an interest–free loan, but to repay this interest-free loan, her older brother Kireet had to work as a Munim for the merchant. Later, the younger generation of Thakur Bhai's family only changed the nomenclature of Munim to 'Office Assistant'.

Her younger brother Uday was fond of Art and was doing a course in Fine Arts. He also was a part of the Bengali Theatre Group. This was not a commercial theatre. Yet, he did manage to occasionally give his mother some money he earned from the sale of his paintings, or from his theatre performance. He looked after his own expenses and this was a big consolation.

Kireet was eligible for marriage but waited for his sister to get married first. His mother used to go after him to get married but each time he declined. There were several proposals from girls' families, but he turned them down. They belonged to a middle-class family. Kirti would have to take up a job after finishing her education, and save up some money for her marriage expenses.

With her MSW Degree, she could have easily got a job in a factory as a Labour welfare Officer or Labour Inspector. As per Labour Laws, it was mandatory for industries to have these posts filled up. Labour Law in Kolkata were implemented very strictly.

Piyush became a frequent visitor to Kirti's house. Once or twice he had met Kireet. Whenever Piyush used to drop Kirti at her house on his bike, Kirti's mother would meet him too. But Kirti did not like the scandalous looks that the neighboring women would give her and so she would have Piyush drop her on the Main road at a short distance from the house. She hated these women's boorish expression.

Kirti had also visited Piyush's house a couple of times. She realized that Piyush's mother was rather brusque and inquisitive; but Piyush insisted so she would visit them occasionally.

Their exams were approaching. Kirti and Piyush would often meet up at the Kalimandir in Kalighat. Kirti thought it was a safe place to meet. It comforted her to pay obeisance to the goddess together with Piyush. She believed that he truly loved her. But he had introduced her to his family as 'Just a college friend'. He had not told them the truth about their relationship.

They would exchange notes and books to prepare for the exam. Her friends lived far away from the college. Piyush had a friend who had rented a room near Bhavanipur, close to her house. This friend hailed from Burdwan and had therefore rented a room in Bhavanipur. Kirti once had been to his room along with a friend. That was the time when she met Piyush and his friend. After they had chatted for a while, Kirti and her friend returned home.

Once Piyush asked her to come to the friend's room to collect a book. She felt a bit awkward about meeting him in a room at that time of the day. Still, she climbed up the stairs to the room on the second floor. For a long time Piyush did not give her the book. She told him that she would leave if he dilly-dallied any longer.

"Don't go, wait. "Here's the book," he said. "Give me a kiss, please." He begged.

She was about to turn to the door, when he held her hand. She looked at him with a frown. He thought she was being coquettish. "Give me a kiss like the one you gave when we were watching a movie at the Odeon theatre." The Hollywood movie they had been watching that day had roused Kirti erotically but today she was in no mood for that.

He let go of her hand and looked at her pleadingly.

"What if someone sees us?"

He took it as an affirmative hint and immediately bolted the door. Then he gently pulled her towards him. He bent his head and gave a light peck on her cheek. He looked into her eyes lovingly. Her eyes didn't respond, neither did she resist. Then he touched her lips, more deliberately this time. She responded passionately. Then she said, "Let me go now."

He said, "Just one more."

"No. That's enough."

He pulled her close to him and held her waist. "Just once," he muttered.

She felt helpless.

He kissed her hard on the lips. He kissed again and again. He put his hands on her back and held her tight.

She begged him to release her from his embrace. He became aggressive. She tried to resist. He held her so tight that her breasts pressed against his chest. He felt a hot desire. He rubbed his chest against her breasts to rouse her. Her resistance proved weak. She muttered, "Piyush, this is not right."

He said, "I feel so passionately in love with you today, I want to get very close to you."

Kirti tried to resist him, to turn him away but he wouldn't relent.

His grip on her loosened a bit and she tried to move to the door quickly but he held her again from behind. He began to kiss her hair, her neck, and her ear lobes. He held her waist tightly with one hand, and with the other he fondled her breasts. She felt a gush of desire and all resistance melted away. He pulled her face to his and showered her with kisses. Both were consumed with passion. He pulled her to the bedstead. She made a mock refusal but now he was in no mood to listen.

He put her on the bed and took her in his arms. He caressed her body with his hands. They didn't realize when their clothes came off their body. She felt the pain of her first sexual experience. Then she moaned and let herself into the sensual pleasure.

Satiated, they came back to their senses. She felt overwhelmed with guilt. She began to cry. "This should not have happened," she said.

"Yes, this shouldn't have happened," he said with a mock guilt. Then with a smile, he said, "Why are you so beautiful? Your face is like a bunch of roses and I felt like kissing each and every rose."

"You are indeed very cunning."

She began to dress and he muttered apologies.

On the third day after this incident, they both rode to the college on his bike to collect their admission card for the exam. On the way back, he asked naughtily if they should go to the friend's room. She punched him on his back playfully.

The exams stretched over a long period of time. He would take her on his bike to the exam center and drop her back home. Her mother and brothers did not object to this because the exams had priority. A week after the exams, Kirti missed her monthly period. She was shocked.

On the pretext of taking a stroll, she came to the Victoria Memorial grounds. She has already telephoned him to meet her there. He was happy that she had called and anticipated an evening full of fun, movies, and so on.

He found her looking grim. He asked her if there was a problem at home.

Tears welled up in her eyes.

"Tell me, what's the matter?"

"There is a problem."

He gave a start." What is it?"

"I am pregnant," she said abruptly.

"My God!" He exclaimed.

He put his hand to his forehead. Both fell silent for a while.

"What must we do now?" He asked.

"We must marry, that's what we must do."

"I don't have a job yet, what shall I tell my family?"

"Tell them whatever you want," she began to sob.

"Look here, stop crying. Other people are watching us."

They were again quiet.

Then he said, "May I ask a question?"

She nodded.

"What if we have it aborted?"

"No. I don't want to have an abortion. I want to get married to you."

"Don't be stubborn. I too want to marry you, you know that. But we need to prepare for that. I need to explain everything to my family."

She said, "That's your concern. You need to decide fast and let me know. Talk to your family."

"I can't muster the courage to do it," he said.

"I don't want to hear any of that nonsense."

"Think over it again. An abortion is the best way out of this problem." He said

"No. I am determined to marry you soon. I do not want to destroy this symbol of our love." She said

"See, try to be sensible. We will meet again tomorrow. You sleep over it. Or perhaps, speak to one of your best friends, take her opinion."

"I am firm in my resolve not to abort our baby."

He became silent.

After some time, he dropped her home on his bike.

The following day, she did not go to the Victoria Memorial Ground. He waited and waited but she did not turn up.

A week passed. He became tense and restless. He went up to her house once. "Let's go for a walk," he suggested.

She asked,"Have you told your family or not?"

He did not answer. She declined to go for a walk with him.

Another month passed. She began to feel sick. She had begun to throw up vomit. Her mother noticed it instantly. She slapped Kirti on her face in a fit of anger. Then she began to cry. Kirti went up to her mother, hugged her and sobbed inconsolably.

The next day, Kirti visited the Kalimandir. She sat there for a long time, thinking about the times she had been there with Piyush. What happy days they were!

She kept thinking about the love between her and Piyush. "Why does a person fall in love? Why is our mind so full of love for someone? What is the source of all this love? I liked Piyush. He was good as a friend. When did I feel this consuming love for him suddenly? Why did I surrender myself so completely to him? What made me want to marry him? Why was I so feeble -minded? Why did I not face the situation courageously? Is love only a union of two minds, or of two bodies? Or a mix of both? What makes us give both our mind and body in an all-consuming love?" Then she began to think of the baby that was growing in her stomach. She considered foeticide a sin. It was a symbol of their love. Why does true love put you to a test? Is my love going to bring misery to my life? She was worried that this love might mar her life forever. She felt afraid of what was going to happen.

Kirti sat in the Kali temple for a long time, immersed in her thoughts. When she realized that other women were looking at her strangely, she felt embarrassed.

She stood up and started walking back home. She reached the Hazra turn. As she walked towards Bhavanipur, she felt uneasy. She reached home and hurried up to the bathroom and vomited. Both her brothers were at home at the time. They thought that some junk food that she ate the previous night with her friends might have caused it. Her mother yelled in anguish, "Go, go have more fun with that Piyush!" When the brothers heard their mother rant, they got an inkling of what must have happened. Kirti laid down on her bed. Perhaps the neighbours had also heard the mother's loud rant and her own retching. Kireet admonished his mother gently." Mother, there is no point in shouting. We have to do something."

"Yes, son, do something. My mind has stopped working."

Kireet asked, "What does Kirti have to say?"

"She insists on marrying Piyush. She does not want an abortion."

"Oh God! Well, I'll talk to her at night. You stay calm. Otherwise the neighbours will get curious." He said.

Both the brothers tried to convince her to have an abortion. She brushed off their suggestion. She was adamant on not doing it. Finally, the brothers decided to meet the Mandal family that Sunday.

Meanwhile, Piyush's father knew some influential people in Howrah. He got Piyush a temporary job as a clerk in a factory in Howrah. Piyush got busy with his job and stopped going over to Kirti's house.

Kirti could not understand this sudden cooling off from Piyush.

When Kirti's brothers and mother called on the Mandals on Sunday, they were asked about their community origins. It was pointed out rather superciliously that they were 'Patels' and not 'Bengali'.

Piyush was not at home at that hour, he was at the factory.

Piyush's mother had seen Kirti before. So the moment Kirti's family came over, she guessed what the matter would be. Kirti's mother directly brought up the topic of marriage and said that Piyush and Kirti were in love.

She did not disclose that Kirti was pregnant.

Piyush's mother said there was no need to hurry. Both had just given their exams and could easily wait for a while.

Kireet said, "We will come again next Sunday."

Mr. Mandal said, "Next time get your daughter along. We would like to see her.

By next Sunday, the Mandals had come to know about Kirti's pregnancy. A nosy neighbor of Kirti had sensed the problem with Kirti. She had guessed that when Kirti's brothers and mother went out, they must have called on the Mandal family. That was it. She took the opportunity to provoke the Mandals with the news. Piyush was admonished severely by his parents. His father called him an idiot. Piyush tried to absolve himself by saying that it was Kirti who had drawn him into a physical relationship.

His father still said he was an idiot having not used a condom.

This started an argument between the mother and father. She said that by suggesting such things he was giving Piyush a free hand to play with other girls' modesty.

Kirti was in a miserable state. Piyush had not shown up at all. Her neighbours would come and meet her and then talk behind her back. She had no intention of going over to meet the Mandals. But she went, only to be insulted by them.

This time Piyush was at home. His mother cast aspersions on her character. Kirti looked helplessly at Piyush, tears streaming down her cheeks. But it failed to touch his heart. In fact, he proved to be a coward. Piyush's mother had no sympathy for the girl. She said with deliberate emphasis, "Such a girl cannot be our daughter-in-law." She said it loud enough for the neighbours to hear.

Kireet was shattered and livid. He said to Piyush's father, "This is not the way decent people behave, (Bhadra Lok-in bangala)"

The father calmed his wife down and putting his palms together he politely asked Kirti's mother to leave and if possible, to forgive them.

Kirti, Kireet and their mother returned home, feeling humiliated. Kirti's mother said harshly, "It would have been better had you not been born. We had lived with our head held high, but you have brought such a shame on us."

Kirti had no other option but to have an abortion. Kirti wept bitterly after the abortion. Her complexion lost its healthy, fair colour. Her eyes sank in. There were dark circles under her eyes making her look older than her age. She became irritable, withdrawn and wilful.

She passed her MSW exam with a first class and learned that Piyush had passed with a second class. Normally, she would have celebrated her success but this time she was indifferent to it.

Three months passed. She lost all hope of Piyush coming into her life again. Then she started looking up vacancies in the newspapers. Howrah city, located across the river, is near Kolkata. Just like Mumbai is near Thane or Pune near Chinchwad. Howrah had a huge industrial estate. She found a job as an Assistant Trainee Labour Welfare, at a plastic bottle manufacturing unit. The owner of this small factory was Nirmal Karwa. Two months passed by smoothly. But from the third month, he started showing his true colours. Not that she was unknown to lascivious looks from males. But her bitter personal experience had made her more perceptive about male glances. She had become self -defensive. She had first mentioned her suspicions about Karwa to her mother.

On the day she received her salary, Karwa made her stay back after office for no reason. He pretended to have some urgent work and asked her to prepare papers for a deal immediately. He went to the factory for a while. She seized that opportunity to dump the finished work on his table and head towards the door. There was a security guard at the door. He was a good man.

From the next day, she stopped attending office. She sent her resignation. Karwa retaliated by saying that she had signed a bond for six months and would therefore have to return three months' salary. She paid no heed to this.

Karwa called up her home and with polite words and asked them for Kirti to resume duty. When she refused, he threatened he would send her a legal notice. Kirti bravely countered him saying she too would send him a notice alleging sexual harassment and put it in the newspaper. This silenced him.

For a couple of months after this incident, Kirti confined herself to her house. The neighouring women harassed her mother. They would taunt her mother about her out–of-marriage pregnancy and abortion. Her mother worried about her prospects for marriage.

Kirti accepted a job at a readymade clothes factory near Dum Dum airport. Although she was the Labour Welfare Assistant as per the Labour Law, she had to manage the entire office administration. There were many women employees there. She had to learn typing and handle the correspondence. The factory was owned by a Bengali couple from Malda. The husband would look after the marketing and the wife would look after the machinery and workers. Kirti had a peaceful; tenure of six months there. By then she had regained her health somewhat. She had become a little carefree. She adopted the metropolitan life-style of Kolkata and dressed smartly. She regained her smart and beautiful look. The neighbours did not stop their sarcastic taunts. Once, when she wore high heeled sandals, they asked her, "Who do you want to trap now, with these smart looks?" She had become very sensitive, touchy and agitated. Since she had got a bad reputation among the acquaintances, no more marriage proposals came for her brothers also. Her mother was annoyed about this matter.

To add to her woes, the factory owner had begun to show an interest in her. The moment she realized this, she went on her guard. She wanted to tell the boss's wife about it. But decided to do so later. She always kept a packet of chilly powder on her person just for self-protection. She had heard about it from a friend but never had to use it. All this factory owner's activities didn't escape the notice of an old experienced lady worker. She immediately told the boss's wife about it. The boss's wife in turn gave Kirti, two months' salary and dismissed her from service. She brazenly told her that she did not want such a beautiful woman working in her factory.

Then Kirti came across the newspaper advertisement by the government enterprise, Ramgadh Coalfields Ltd. She applied for it and also attended an interview. There was a lot of argument over this at home. She had told her family very clearly that the pay would be good in a government job and she would send part of her salary to home for them. She would no longer have to search for jobs. The truth was that she was fed up of living in Kolkata. When the appointment letter arrived, she reported on duty to a place that was at quite a distance from Kolkata.

She did not realize how much time had elapsed in her reverie. It had become dark. She could see the glimmer of evening lights in Maraal. In five minutes, her rickshaw drove up in front of her living quarters. She got off and walked towards the door. Baldev picked up the purse she had left behind in the rickshaw and walked into the house behind her.

Madan Oza was sitting in his Depot. There were two trucks being loaded with coal. Both trucks were headed for the Mughalsarai coal market. Mughalsarai or Benares Coal Market was a well-known coal market in Uttar Pradesh state, from where coal would be supplied to the rest of Uttar Pradesh, Delhi, Haryana and Punjab states. Mughalsarai market would receive both legitimate supplies as well as black market supply of coal. Coal from the Midnapur Mine of Bengal would also reach Mughalsarai.

Ramnaresh Yadav reached the Depot on his motorcycle. He got off and wiped his face with his gamchha (scarf). Then he dusted his kurta with the scarf. He stomped around in his heavy, black, miner shoes. He asked one of the loaders, "Where is your boss?" The worker pointed towards a cabin.

Madan Oza had recognized Ramnaresh's bike vrooming into the loading area. He was already standing at the door of his cabin when Ramnaresh stepped in.

"Welcome Pehelwanji (Wrestler)"

Ramnaresh greeted him with a Namaste. There were four cabins in the office. One of the rooms, which Madan used as a bedroom, was locked. Madan took him into an air -conditioned cabin and ordered the peon to get some tea and snacks (samosas).

Ramnaresh asked him why he had sent for him.

"Is your dairy business doing alright?" Madan asked.

"Yes. Business is fine. There are eight buffalos. I will be getting two more next month."

"How many people are there to help you?"

"Two. One is Naval Prasad and the other is Suresh Singh." Ramnaresh replied.

"And there must be a impersonator (Baniharee) working instead of you on the site, so now you have plenty leisure time." Madan said

Ramnaresh smiled sheepishly.

"Will you work for me?" Madan queried.

"What kind of work?" Ramnaresh asked.

He used to meet Madan Oza often because Oza was from his hometown and a rich man as well. But they never had any business dealing before.

"Are you saying that you refuse to accept unless you know the nature of work?"

"No, not that way Sir,"Ramnaresh hesitated.

"Look, I am not asking you to commit a murder or get into a scuffle."

Ramnaresh looked at him with curiosity.

"Look, we need someone to supervise the loading of coal into our trucks at the Maraal Siding. Our regular man has gone to his native place, Baliya, to look into some problem about his farm. We don't know whether he will return."

Ramnaresh quickly remarked, "Oh, this is the kind of job,I will be happy to serve you."

Madan Oza placed his hand on Ramnaresh's shoulder. Both had a well-toned, strong physique. Ramnaresh didn't feel the weight of Oza's arm on his shoulder.

Ramnaresh joined his hands and bowed slightly.

Just then, the peon brought in the tea and samosas. Madan offered it to Ramnaresh.

After the repast, Ramnaresh got up to leave.

"You did not ask me what your remuneration would be." Oza said.

"I will be satisfied with whatever you pay."

Madan Oza briefed him, "Look, I have sent Manik Prasad there. Go and meet him. I will inform Manik tonight. You meet him tomorrow. Take the money meant for workers' wages from him. He will make a note of it in his diary. You need not come to Ramgadh to collect the workers' wages. Manik will himself hand it over to you every second or third day. If required, you may have to put in the money yourself. You must keep a record of how many trucks have been loaded and the truck number. At the end of every month, you will be paid for per truck loaded".

Ramnaresh looked at him longingly.

"Don't worry. I will pay you well."

Madan told Ramnaresh that he had seen the loading process a month and a half ago. He asked if there had been any changes since then.

"No, nothing has changed. How can it improve? Ashok Kumar is interested only in making more money. It was the same with the Sales Manager, Deepak Chaterjee. They load most of the good quality coal into the Railway Siding. The major portion of the underground coal goes there. Some of the underground coal reaches us at the Maraal Siding, but the dumpers also dump some newly started opencast mine coal here, which has some stones in it."

Madan said, "Well, okay. We must ensure that good quality coal is loaded otherwise we will not get a good price. If required, you must quietly steal superior quality coal from the Railway Siding. We must load only superior quality coal into our trucks for sure."

"Yes, Sir." He affirms and asks" "May I leave now?"

Madan Oza says, "Okay."

Ramnaresh asks, "What about the money to be paid to the bosses there?"

"At this moment, I am not giving you that responsibility. I am handling that matter myself. You continue to work there and once they are convinced that you are our trusted man, then we can think about it."

Ramnaresh nodded his head and departed.

Santosh Kumar Sinha, Project Officer hosted a party at the Guest House in Maraal on Saturday. He had invited some special officers from Ichotu Area and some officers from Headquarters. Satish Trivedi had already reached there. The reason for the party was to express his gratitude for saving him from being beaten up by the mine workers on the day of the mishap in the mine. He also wanted to settle all ruffled feathers and see that the nexus was as used to be before. So he had invited a large number of guests. There were officers belonging to the Vigilance and Security Department of Headquarters, Ramgadh Coalfields. Ramesh Varma, Vigilance officer was also an invitee. All of them were either middle or lower rung Officials. There was the Staff Officer and the Deputy General Manager from the Ichotu Area Office. The General Manager had deliberately not been invited as a precautionary measure as there was no guarantee what someone might blabber under the influence of alcohol. Satish Trivedi felt he was the only General Manager there. The guests were trickling in. The party had started early on the pretext that Satish Trivedi wanted to leave early. In a while, there were quite a few guests. Since the following day was a Sunday, everyone was rather relaxed. Ramesh Varma downed his drinks fast, so one of the officers asked him to go slow and stuffed some paneer tikka into his mouth.

Santosh Kumar had arranged for a lavish spread. There was chicken tikka, fried fish, fried cashew nuts, onion fritters, assorted mixture or farsan and some fruit pieces. There was a variety of liquor— Royal Challenge whisky and Old Monk Rum and Beer.

Every time a new guest walked in, glasses were topped up again to a fresh round of 'Cheers!' If someone still had a drink in his glass, he would only raise his glass to say 'Cheers!' Santosh Kumar poured very small pegs for himself. Ashok Kumar Jha was responsible for the smooth conduct of the party, and he was doing a good job with the help of Deepak Chatterjee, the Sales Manager. Ramesh Varma had heard the Security Officer from Area Headquarters narrating the tragic incident at the mine field to everyone in detail. Ramesh said to Mr. Sinha, "Actually, those two women saved your skin, don't you agree Prabhunath?"

Prabhunath felt compelled to agree.

Neeraj Kumar quiped, "Those two women should have been invited to the party!"

One of the guests said, "What would the two women have done here? A cabaret dance?" Every one laughed.

Prabhunath shut up that guest politely.

Satish Trivedi became cautious. He felt the guests already had a few drinks and were getting lewd. There was every chance that one of them might taunt him in jest about his philandering. So he shook hands with everyone and left the party. Project Manager Sinha and Deepak Chaterjee escorted him to his car.

The topic of conversation veered towards impersonators (Baniharees). By then Ramesh Varma was very drunk. He avered, "Let the Baniharee custom continue. I will handle it. You just send me the money regularly. I will tip you off about any surprise vigilance checks. You don't worry about anything." By then he spread himself on the sofa.

The officials from headquarters watched Varma's antics in amazement. They said that four months ago, Ramesh Varma had created quite a scene at Chhitarpur under the influence of liquor. Varma heard these words and muttered," What did I do? I did nothing." He again collapsed on the sofa, totally drunk.

Neeraj Kumar declared that the custom of impersonator (Baniharee) labour would decline over the years and they all had to make a concerted effort to stop it.

He was seconded by Satpal singh, another Vigilance Officer from Headquarters. He said that such exploitation of the poor Baniharee must stop and they must be shown sympathy.

Area Personnel Manager Narenkumar said, "The practice is not going to stop just by our saying it. Those who hire impersonators (Baniharees) do it with money power; and those who agree to work do it are primitives from the jungles here, or they come from Orissa or Bengal."

Prabhunath agreed. He said, "Yes, there are places like Kalahandi in Orissa. There is severe mal-nutrition there. People have no work, and no food. They come here in search of work. The same is true of Bengal."

The Personnel Manager from Headquarters said, "I think we have had enough of Baniharee talk. It will dilute all the alcohol we have consumed and snap us back into reality."

Everyone laughed out aloud.

Sinha insisted on another round of drinks. Dinner was announced. Nobody had much of an appetite after the lavish hors d 'oeu vres.

Dinner was sumptuous. Chicken curry and fish curry were special items. There was paneer –matar (Cottage cheese and pea curry), potato-cauliflower veggie. There were rotis and naans (Wheat breads), plain rice and pulav. There were assorted desserts like Rasgullas, Gulabjamun, Kheerkadam, ice-cream and paan as well.

Sinha was urging everyone to indulge in the food. Ashok Kumar and Deepak Chaterjee were also playing generous hosts to all.

Ramesh Varma had been served a small portion of Pulav rice. He was just pecking at it. He gulped down another peg. Then he went into the bathroom and vomited. Then he came back and sank on the sofa again. Whisky was being offered during dinner too. One or two guests accepted and were enjoying their drinks.

The chauffers of the cars had been served dinner too. But they had been given only a single peg each to drink.

The party came to an end. Each of the guests departed thanking Sinha profusely for the party and Sinha in turn thanked them for attending the occasion.

The Officers from Headquarters had to do the difficult task of heaving Ramesh Varma up from the sofa and making him walk to his waiting car. He was handed over to his driver to be driven back home in his inebriated state. Satpal Singh said that this had become a regular feature with Ramesh Varma. "We warn him not to drink too much before coming to a party, he promises not to and then forgets his promise and gets drunk and sprawls all over the place. We have to do the dirty work afterwards."

A fortnight later there was another vigilance raid at the Maraal loading point. This time Headquarters had taken a firm step and sent a Deputy Chief Personnel Manager and a Security Officer with the team. The team had to take some stern steps. The Project had been tipped off about it.

Madan Oza had asked Ramnaresh Yadav to go to Mughalsarai on the truck. Ramnaresh was not at the site the previous evening so he could not be informed. Kirti had to attend a meeting in Ichotu Area office so she too had no idea about the raid. Naval Prasad, Ramnaresh's henchman, had not been told in order to keep the information secret. Janu Prasad had gone to his village to work on his fields.

Jaggu Manjhi and Kali Manjhi had become suspicious when they noticed that other Baniharee workers had not come on duty. But many times previously the warning about vigilance raid had turned out to be a false alarm. There would be no raid. Besides, Jaggu was not going to budge unless he had instructions from Ramnaresh as he did not want to miss out on his salary in case the checking did not happen at all.

This time, Ramesh Varma was not on the vigilance team. Instead there was another officer and Satpal Singh. Kirti got the intimation about the raid quite late in the day. By then the checking was done. This time there were four officers in place of two, so the checking was done faster. Jaggu Manjhi and Kali Manjhi had been trapped. As Ramnaresh and Janu Prasad were supposed to be on the muster roll that day, it was obvious that Jaggu and Kali were substituting for them as impersonators (Baniharees). Neither possessed any identity card and were working at a government site.

Ashok Kumar and Kirti Patel tried to convince the vigilance team to quash the case. The Deputy Chief Personnel Manager on the team had been transferred here from another coal company. He wasn't familiar with the happenings here and considered the case very serious. Satpal Singh told him to try to treat it more leniently. But it was a difficult task to convince the entire team to take a milder stand on the issue. Prabhunath Singh hinted at a bribe, but could not say it openly. Ashok Kumar and Deepak talked to Satpal Singh about money but Satpal was afraid that the Deputy Chief Personnel Manager might report his dishonesty to Headquarters.

Headquarters at Ramgadh had made a decision to inspect all the projects and coal fields and issued orders for stern action to be taken in case of discrepancies. So each one of the four members on the team was playing safe. They were not able to come to a joint decision about a compromise on the impersonation (Baniharee) issue. Each one was worried that he might be held guilty in case the compromise was exposed. Prabhunathsingh and Deepak Chatergee tried to convince the team, that this may be taken as a stray or rare case and be leniently absolved, but the team members were hesitant.

Besides, in the absence of Ramnaresh and Janu Prasad, there was no one to directly plead for leniency and to make a cash offer. Jaggu and Kali were too bewildered to say anything.

Ashok Kumar, Prabhunath Singh, and Deepak Chaterjee had to put their signature on the report made by the team. Prabhunath Singh was in charge as Project Officer, Sinha was on leave.

The team returned to Headquarters.

Ramnaresh got to know of the incident when he returned the next day. He got his men to beat up Jaggu mercilessly for letting himself be caught.

Within the next four days, punitive action was taken on the basis of the report. Ramnaresh and Janu Prasad were suspended from duty and instructions for an inquiry against them were initiated.

By the end of the week, someone from Area Office handed over the suspension orders.

Jaggu Manjhi fell on bad days again. He looked about for a job. When he tried to find a job as a truck loader, Ramnaresh had ensured that he did not get the job. But the Jaggu got acquainted with a Sikh supervisor, who worked for the transporter at Dhanbad. He took pity on Jaggu. When Ramnaresh picked up a quarrel with him over Jaggu, the Sardarji flashed his Kirpan (a long knife). This cowed down Ramnaresh's men. Ramnaresh couldn't do anything. Jaggu got the job. But the wages were very poor, just Rs100 per day.

Radha had found two more domestic help jobs to make both ends meet. She would be dead -beat by the time she returned home from work. Jaggu's main worry was the repayment of the loan he had taken for his family in Kundapara. He had taken it at an interst rate of 10% per month. He had put his thumb impression on a stamp paper. If he defaulted on the interest in any month, then it would be added into his original loan. The amount kept increasing and the interest as well.

Ramnaresh's used his suspension as an excuse not to pay Jaggu that month's salary. Jaggu was therefore unable to pay that month's interest of Rupees 1200.00. The money-lender kept pestering him. He knew that Jaggu had been removed from his job as a wagonloader. So now he was insisting on getting back the full amount. Jaggu had begged him to give him some more grace time to repay the loan.

Jaggu worked harder on the coal loading. Sometimes he would earn a little extra money. In the mornings, he would help Radha. He took upon himself the chore of fetching water from the river.

Other women would tease him a little. By helping her with the chores, he was able to save her a little time. She had to make his breakfast and lunch early and she too was able to leave for work early to cope with the extra load she had taken on.

Ramnaresh was a worried man now, because of suspension. If the inquiry against him held him guilty, he would be dismissed and it would be impossible to continue living in Maraal. He had already made himself comfortable in Maraal by extending his allotted quarters. He had a cow-shed built in his back and front yards. He had got his compound enclosed with a brick wall. He had made cement benches for his henchmen to sit on. He had treated his allotted quarters like his private property. He was the major milk supplier in the colony. He supplied milk free of cost to the families of Prabhunath Singh, Ashok Kumar and Deepak Chaterjee. So he was in the good books of the officers. He had requested all the officers to have his suspension orders withdrawn. They had assured him they would do something but nothing had been done so far.

Ramnaresh approached Madan Oza. Oza promised him that he would do the needful and asked him to concentrate on the coal loading.

Oza had visited Ramgadh headquarters and the Area Office. An inquiry Officer had not yet been appointed. The inquiry was going to take place at the Area level. Oza succeeded in having the inquiry put on hold for a while and got Ramnaresh and Janu Prasad to join duty pending inquiry. Oza was going to recover the expenses incurred on this account from Ramnaresh and Janu Prasad.

Ramnaresh had to load the coal himself on the day he resumed duty and on the following day too. Janu Prasad also had to load it himself. Then they began to search for Jaggu and Kali Manjhi. Kali Manjhi immediately agreed to work. But Jaggu refused to work. Ramnaresh had managed to convince Ashok Kumar to sanction some leave. Actually, he found it physically difficult to lift the coal –filled baskets and hoist them into the rail wagons because his body that had been on milk- rich diet had become heavy. He would get tired very soon.

Ramnaresh tried with the help of two of his musclemen, to threaten Jaggu into coming back to work. But they were thwarted by the Sardarji. Ramnaresh even tried to coax Suresh Singh, his henchman to work as Baniharee, but to no avail.

When all attempts to get Jaggu back to work failed, Ramnaresh used his ace card. He told Jaggu that he would give him the wages he was due during Ramnaresh's suspension period. Jaggu was already being dogged by the money-lender. The thought of so much money tempted him. The Sardarji tried to warn him but Jaggu was lured into the trap by Ramnaresh. Jaggu had asked for a raise of fifty rupees per day in his wages and Ramnaresh agreed to it, Because Ramnaresh no longer had the stamina to lift the heavy coal baskets himself.

Radha did not like the idea of Jaggu going back to impersonator (Baniharee) work. But Jaggu reminded her about the debt repayment. He once again went back to doing slave–labour. Their mind would oscillate between going back to Kundapara and staying in Maraal. They continued to live in their dilemma. Jaggu knew very well that till he does not repay his loan, he can not escape from this place.

Jaggu would meet Ramlal at the work place or outside. Jaggu would generally avoid going to Ramlal's house. He would call out to Ramlal, "Uncle (Chachaji)!" and together they would go to a wayside tea stall to have a cup of tea. It was Ramlal who would pay for the tea. He welcomed a chance to be able to chit-chat with someone.

That day too their chat lasted a long time.

Ramlal said Jaggu should not have gone back to work for that bastard Ramnaresh again. Jaggu had to tell him about the loan he had taken from the money-lender. Ramlal was aware of it, but he had to be reminded again.

Ramlal said, "Get rid of this debt as soon as you can. It is a vicious circle that entraps a man. One should never take a loan, especially from wicked money lenders. "

Jaggu told him that he had to take the loan out of desperation.

Ramlal agreed. He said, "Yes, you were desperate. But my son Shivlal was not. He wanted to live beyond his means, like a big officer. Thank God, he had taken a bank loan. After Shivlal's death, I had to repay it."

Jaggu commiserates with him. "Yes, you all had to bear a lot of hardships, Chachiji, and especially Pârbati Bhabhi..."

"Yes. We all had to suffer. I never imagined our daughter-in-law Pârbati would have to suffer so much. It is all my fault. I should never have insisted." Said Ramlal.

"What did you insist on?"

"I was bent on giving my son higher education for making him a big officer. It's Parbati's misfortune. What else?"

Ramlal was lost in the memories. Many times, he would lapse into the past in the middle of a chat. Jaggu knew most of the events in Ramlala's life, but sometimes he heard something new.

The story of Ramlal, Janaki and Parbati was a strange one. It revolved around Shivlal. But Shivlal had gone to his heavenly abode.

Parbati had come into the house as a ten-year old bride. Shivlal was thirteen years old at the time. He was studying in class VII. Parbati's maiden home was Kodarma village, ahead of Hazaribaug.

Ramlal lived in a shanty at the time. He and Janaki worked in the coalmine. It was before coalmines were nationalized. Railway wagons would arrive at Maraal for loading of the coal and Janaki and Ramlal worked as loaders. It was Ramlal's dream to educate his son and make him an official, not be a coal loader like his father.

When Parbati came into the family, she had Kunti, her sister-in-law, for company. Kunti and Parbati were of the same age and Ramlal had put both of them to work at the coal-loading point. They would fill up the baskets with coal and Ramlal and Janaki would pick them up and load the coal into the waiting wagons.

The wages earned were not much. But more the number of family members working, more were the collective wages. So everyone except Shivlal went to work.

Every Sunday the ritual of drinking alcohol would be followed. They belonged to the Khakhar Adivasi (Primitive) Tribe. This was an age-old tradition and everyone from the young to the old would drink as a custom. There would be goat or buffalo meat for lunch on Sunday. The only exception was when there was a wedding or a funeral; on such occasions, the drinking would continue for two-three days.

Shivlal would find his wife's going to work very funny. He would tease her about it. Sometimes she would get annoyed at his teasing. Shivlal was good at studies. He would study hard and be the first or second in his class. He would start studying soon after returning from school. He avoided having to study by the light of a lantern. His father, Ramlal, had impressed upon his mind from a very early age that he would not be a coalmine worker. He topped his school in the matriculation examination. He was in a hurry to start earning. He visited the coalfield office twice or thrice. But he could not get the job.

The supervisor of Ramlal, who hailed from Ranchi, was a kind, elderly man. He advised Ramlal to send his son to a polytechnic college for further education so that he could get a supervisor's job with that qualification.

Ramlal remarked that the expenses would be too much.

Nathuram Singh, supervisor said that there would be a little expense, but he could also hope for a scholarship and concession in the fee. He said that since Ramlal belonged to a Scheduled Tribe, Shivlal was entitled to a waiver of fees. And since Shivlal was a bright student, he would also get a scholarship. Since Shivlal was already getting a small scholarship at school, Ramlal was aware of such a provision.

At first Shivlal was not inclined to go all the way to Ranchi. But Janaki and Parbati insisted. By that time, his second sister Kunti was married and was at her husband's place. He was very embarrassed that his father, mother and wife were persuading him to continue his higher education. Eventually, he agreed and took up a course in Electrical engineering.

Parvati was sixteen years old by then. She was dark but had attractive features. She looked mature and grown up. She had a healthy physique and a well-toned body because of hard physical work.

Shivlal still looked boyish in comparison.

Shivlal began to put on more muscle when he entered college. He would come home in the vacations and now his conjugal relationship with Parbati took on a new, sensuous turn.

When Shivlal was in his second year of college, the coal mines were nationalized. Parbati was yet to attain the age of eighteen but Ramlal had managed to show she was eighteen and got her a permanent job in the coalmine. Ramlal and Janaki already held permanent jobs. When all three of them started to earn government wages, their financial condition improved considerably. This had a very marked impact on Shivlal's life style. He began to dress differently. Parbati worked hard to ensure that her husband had a good lifestyle.

She once casually asked him if he got a chance to drink liquor in Ranchi. He said that his classmates belonged to the upper caste, middle class families and were not in the habit of consuming alcohol in the house. There were one or two friends from the tribal caste but they now lived in the city. Although they did not mind anyone drinking, Shivlal had not told any of his friends about the Adivasi custom of drinking on Sundays at home.

When Shivlal was in the third year, he sired a daughter. He wanted to give her a modern name like Nutan or Vaijayanti, but his mother insisted on the name being Lakshmi.

By the year in which he obtained his Diploma, all the vacancies in the coalmine had been filled up. He wished to take up a job in some factory in Tatanagar or Ranchi, but his family objected his going so far from home. So he had to accept the post of a Trainee Foreman at the coalmine on a monthly stipend of Rs.150/-

Within a year, he became a foreman at a monthly salary of Rs.450/-. He would urge his family to give up their jobs as he earned a decent salary, which would also increase over the years. As he was at the Supervisory level, he felt it demeaning for his family to do menial work as wagon loaders. Another daughter was born. Shivlal wanted to name her Hema or Rekha, but yet again Janaki's wish prevailed and the girl was named Saraswati. Janaki gave up her job to look after her two granddaughters. There was a lot of support from home.

Two years ago, Ramlal and Parbati had been allotted individual quarters, adjacent to one another. They had demolished the portion of adjoining wall and put a door between the two quarters. So it now became a large house with four to five rooms. They no more had to worry about a leaking roof of hut in the rainy season. The birth of his son coincided with his promotion to the post of Foreman-in-charge. This time, Shivlal was very happy that he was allowed to have his way in naming his son, 'Manoj', a name he liked. Shivlal had begun to earn a decent salary by then. But he had also taken to drinking alcohol outside the house in the company of his colleagues. Sometimes he would return home late in the night. He had developed a taste for imported liquor rather than the Indian brews. Parbati was the first person to object to this but he paid no heed. She told her mother-in-law, who in turn tried to convince her son not to get addicted. She said as they were having alcohol every Sunday, an excess of it would ruin his health and so on. Shivlal promised her that he would give it up.

Eight years had passed. First an Engineer, then Executive Engineer, Shivlal climbed up the ladder. He was allotted the bigger 'B' type quarters. Father Ramlal retained the miners' quarters for storing junk. Parbati had given up her job. She learned to read and write a bit along with Manoj. Over a period of time she was able to read the local Hindi newspaper. She socialized with the wives of Shivlal's colleagues. She would command due respect as the wife of the Executive Engineer. But behind her back, a few women would snigger over her lack of education and her past menial work as a wagon loader. However, the wives of the officers, supervisors and foremen were cordial with Parbati as she was a down-to-earth, humble sort of person.

One day, Shivlal went on a trip with his colleagues to celebrate his promotion as Executive Engineer. The location was the Chhinnamastika Devi Temple at Rajarappa. Although it was a Sunday, Shivlal had abstained from drinking as he was on a visit to the temple. He was sober and in a convivial mood that day.

That night Parbati asked him, "What have you decided?"

He was taken aback. "What about?" He asked. "About our son's education and daughter's marriage?"

Shivlal was feeling sleepy. He said, "With God's grace everything will happen in good time."

She remarked, "God's blessings are always there. But humans also have to make efforts."

"I don't understand."

"I am talking about your excessive drinking. If you are going to waste all our money on drinking and eating, how will we save up for our daughter's marriage? We have come up the very hard way. We had to cope with leaking roofs in hut, fetch water from the river. Ought we to forget all this? If we have reached a better position today, should we not retain it?"

He was a bit irritated. He said, "Did you have to bring up this topic today, of all days?"

She said nothing. She thought that on other days he was rarely sober enough to talk about it.

The next day onwards Shivlal was back to his boozing. Life went on as before.

Maraal had an enormous stock of underground coal. A new district was to start in the new underground number 4. 'District', in coalmining jargon meant the digging up of a new coal area in a new direction and level. A new batch of workers had been brought in from Chhitarpur and Chutkakhana mines.

Shivlal was in charge of the electrical work. He was busy with wiring, pumping and also laying of the cables. The work was exhausting and it affected his health. His drinking continued unabated. The scope of this work brought him in contact with suppliers and contractors from whom he made a little extra money. But even this money was wasted on liquor.

It took two years for the new underground development to complete. In this period, Pârbati's house had got a complete makeover. There was a new sofa set, double bed, TV and Fridge. Shivlal continued with his drinking habit. He suffered from blood pressure.

His job became more demanding. He began to have tiffs with his mother. Any talk of liquor would rile him up.

One Sunday, he felt unwell and lay in his bed. Parbati suggested a visit to the doctor. Shivlal said that the government clinic would be closed on Sunday. She suggested going to the doctor's house. He refused and said he would consult a doctor the following day. The next day she wanted him to take leave to visit the doctor but he again refused and said he would go to the doctor on his way back from office in the afternoon. That was the end. He never came back after that.

He had a massive heart attack at the mine. He died before he could be taken to the hospital. The mine staff performed the last rites.

The untimely death of young, main earning member of family brings so much misery to the family members. The shocks and aftershocks are tremendous. It is taken for granted always, that the main earning member will be with them till his old age. The suddun realization of helplessness and deep grief makes that family vunerable to mental depression.

Ramlal was burdened with a different kind of responsibility. He was the only earning member in the family now. Parbati was in a miserable state. It was feared she might lose control over her senses. Ramlal sent for his daughter and had her stay for over a month. Pârbati's brother's wife, Madhu, also spent a few days with the bereaved family. Both these girls stood by Parbati giving her the necessary support to bear her loss. It took two-three months for Parbati to come to terms with her life. She applied for a job at the office of the coalmine. They had to vacate the Engineers' quarters following Shivlal's death. They sold off all the bulky furniture including the TV, sofa, double bed and fridge. Ramlal had repaid almost all the bank loans. He was not willing to let Parbati work again. But she prevailed upon him to allow her to work, as one day he too would retire and her job would be a great help.

On compassionate grounds, Parbati was given a labour job. But instead of loading coal she was asked to work as a peon in the office. The people to whose houses, Parbati used to visit as the wife of an Executive Engineer, she now worked in their office running errands for them. She had to serve tea and water, deliver the mail. When she made a mistake in delivering the mail to the right department, the clerical staff would scold her for not knowing English. Only Kirti Patel had a kind disposition towards her. With the passage of time, Parbati got used to the office routine.

That day Ramlal had again immersed himself in the sad memories of his son. He came out of his reverie when Jaggu asked him whether they should get up and leave. He said, "Yes Jaggu. Let's go."

Both of them walked to their respective homes.

On the way home, it occurred to Jaggu that Ramlal was still very grounded. Only his dreams were lofty. His son had become a high ranking official but he had stuck on to his job as a loader. On the other hand, Parbati Bhabi had climbed great heights and her misfortune had flung her down to earth from sky.

There was another meeting in the Commissioner's office at Hazaribaug that day. The Coordinator of the meeting was the Deputy Collector and everyone was handing over their data-sheets to him. When Renuka Mane and Kripal Singh handed over their sheets to him, he warned them to be careful in their remarks that day because two senior officers from State ministry, Ranchi, one from the Home Ministry and the other from the Tribal Welfare Ministry were going to be present. All the officials had received specific instructions from that deputy collector, so the atmosphere at the meeting was quite solemn. Each Officer had presented his case very emphatically in front of the Ministry officials. Kripal Singh and Renuka Mane stated the problems and the developments in their areas. This time there was no argument between them. The Commissioner looked satisfied and calm. Lunch was arranged at the PWD (Public Works Department) Guest House. It was a pure vegetarian menu full of all vegetarian dishes and the lunch lasted an hour and a half.

Everyone was back in their seats after lunch. They were all feeling a bit lethargic. The coordinator started projecting all the collected data on the screen. Everyone had been given Xerox sheets of the same so it was easy to look at the screen and the sheet on their table. The Commissioner gave some suggestions. Once or twice, the officers from the Ministries gave suggestions and instructions. The meeting concluded very peacefully.

Kripal Singh noticed outside the office that Renuka Mane's chauffer was pushing the jeep forward with the help of other drivers. Renuka was very annoyed with the driver for not maintaining the jeep well. He explained that the previous week he had got the self-starter repaired yet it was giving a problem. Kripal Singh approached Renuka and offered to drop her in his vehicle.

Renuka declined saying that if her jeep broke down again, two people would be required to push it. The Jeep had to reach Ramgadh somehow as it was unsafe for a police jeep to be stranded in the midst of a Naxal (terrorist) area in Khuru Valley.

Kripal Singh told her that he would ask his driver to sit in her jeep. His vehicle would follow her jeep. And if she agreed they could have a cup of coffee at a wayside inn and then go ahead.

Renuka realized that Kripal Singh was trying to use the opportunity to get close with her. But the situation was such that she couldn't refuse. So without further hesitation, she let her jeep go ahead.

Kripal Singh and Renuka stoped for a cup of coffee at some coffee house. There they met Mr. and Mrs. Gokhale. Renuka introduced Kripal Singh to them and narrated the jeep incident to them. Mr. Gokhale invited them to sit at their table and picked up the tab (bill payment) himself despite protestations from Kripal Singh.

Mr. Gokhale told Kripal Singh that he is an old patron of the coffee house so the proprietor would heed his word, not Kripal Singh's. At Hazaribaug, he would play the host and Renuka and Kripal were his honoured guests. Kripal Singh felt elated because in Jharkhand and Bihar, the son-in-law would also be referred to as 'honored guest (mehman)'.

After coffee, they bade good-bye to the Gokhales. Kripal Singh speeded up his car. She told him there was no need to drive that fast.

He said they needed to catch up with the police jeep. She agreed, still he slowed down a little after that.

They talked about the Administrative Staff College at Dehradun. Renuka had been trained there for a while and then joined the Police Academy at Hyderbad. It turned out that one of Kripal Singh's friends, Damodaran, by name, had married one of

Renuka's friends, Priya Ganguly. Renuka had not been in contact with Priya in recent times, but Kripal was very much in touch with Damodaran.

Kripal Singh told her that he would always tease Damodaran that he should have chosen to work in Jharkhand cadre so he would always have worked on the banks of the Damodar river.

Renuka smiled at this.

Kripal Singh was to give Renuka, Damodaran's phone number so that she could get in touch with Priya. On sighting the jeep ahead of them, Kripal Singh slowed down his car. They had already passed through the dangerous Khuru valley by then. Both could now talk to each other in a more relaxed way.

In a room at the Park Hotel in Park Street at Kolkata, Piyush Mandal and Satish Trivedi were enjoying their booze party. It was Friday night. Trivedi had a meeting with the West Bengal Electricity Board officials on Thursday and Friday. Kolkata was facing a terrible power shortage those days. The WBEB (West Bengal Electricity Board) officials had visited Ramgadh earlier for a meeting. Power shortage would become a government issue because coalmine officials and the ministry would start a blame game via newspapers and other media. Kolkata newspapers would play a leading role. The leaders of the various political parties would also be very vociferous. So the Managing Director and other officers at Ramgadh Coalfields had to handle the Electricity Board officers very carefully. There would always be arguments over coal linkages and the grading of coal.

The results of the RCL coal samples about quality would never correlate with the result of the Board Lab. There would be a lot of letter-exchange on both sides over this issue. So a committee had been constituted under the leadership of Trivedi. The Electricity Board had been demanding that a meeting be held in Kolkata. Trivedi was in Kolkata to attend this meeting. He was to be accompanied by a Deputy Chief Finance Manager. This man had fallen ill at the last moment and Trivedi had to come alone.

Trivedi loved to come alone because it gave him all the liberty to indulge in his favorite activities.

Piyush Mandal was the Administrative Officer at the Board He had been asked to liaise with Trivedi. Mandal had declared at the very beginning that he did not hold a very high post and could therefore not spend lavishly on entertaining Trivedi.

Trivedi had said that money did not matter; he only wanted good company.

Both were a little tipsy after downing two pegs each. Trivedi wanted to get Piyush Mandal to the heart of the matter of availability of prostitutes, but he could not muster the courage to do it.

Piyush kept on saying, "Go slow, Sir. One can enjoy one's drinks only by sipping it slowly."

To avoid bringing up the topic of the prostitute abruptly, Trivedi asked Mandal about his family, how many children he had.

Mandal told him that he has two daughters. And how many did Trivedi have?

Trivedi told him that he has two sons.

Trivedi asked him casually whether it had been a love marriage. Piyush very casually replied that he did not have a love marriage.

Trivedi took a dig at him by asking, "Well not a love marriage, but you did make love?"

"Yes, I did. But I ditched her, or rather; she was cheated by my parents."

"It must have saddened you a lot?" Trivedi said.

"Yes, it made me very sad. She did not deserve such a treatment. Besides, she was pregnant." Piyush said.

"Do you remember her often?"

"I have almost forgotten her now. But when I see a tragic movie, her face flashes across my mind."

Just then the waiter knocked at the door to take their lunch order.

Trivedi placed the order. He asked Mandal if he would like some fish curry. Mandal replied that since they just had some fried fish, there was no need for another fish dish. As Trivedi liked chicken, he could order a chicken dish. The waiter took the order.

The topic switched back to 'women'.

"May I ask you a personal question, Sir?" Asked Mandal.

"What is it?" Enquired Trivedi

"About being in love?"

Trivedi winked at Mandal and says, "Oh, my love affairs, you mean? I had plenty of them. But I never got seriously involved in any. I love to have flings. I believe in the formula, 'Use and Throw'."

He put his glass to his lips.

"Then how do you manage the domestic scene?" Mandal asked

"My wife is an understanding lady. She has an inkling of my dalliances, but she never utters a word." Told Trivedi

"That's very nice," Mandal said.

Now Trivedi came to the point. "Can't I get a call girl here in Kolkata?"

Mandal was speechless. He said he doesn't know much as he had never indulged in such things.

Trivedi said to him that surely he would be having a friend or someone who knew about such things.

Mandal was a bit flustered. This was something unexpected. In his capacity as a liaison officer to Trivedi, he had been asked to look after Trivedi's needs. Many times, he had arranged for a taxi to take Trivedi from the office to the hotel room or for an outing. But this was a different 'Taxi' that Trivedi demanded.

Mandal wished to refuse straight away and tell Trivedi that arranging for a one -night fling was not in his line of duty. But he was drunk and couldn't gather enough courage to do so. Trivedi had entertained him with good food and drinks. He felt awkward about turning down Trivedi's request outright.

He assured Trivedi that he would do his best to find someone.

Trivedi told him to try hard and make arrangements for the next day.

Piyush assured him that he would do his best.

Trivedi told him that if not in the afternoon, he could get someone for the night, perhaps in the hotel room itself.

Mandal said that it was impossible to do so in that five-star hotel room. If, at the time of check-in, Trivedi had brought along a lady companion, she could have been registered as his wife. Now it was against hotel rules to send in a lone female guest for the night to stay.

Trivedi asked him how he knew these procedures. Mandal told him that he had heard it from a driver. What he did not tell Trivedi is that he had heard about it during an incident involving another RCL officer in a similar situation.

Trivedi told Mandal to seek out the driver who would of course know several addresses to get a call girl for him.

After dinner, Mandal asked Trivedi if he would need a car the next day.

Trivedi said he would need a car at noon to attend a lunch hosted by his friend at Baligunj. Later on he would like Mandal to meet him at 4 pm.

Mandal said he would be there at 4pm.

Trivedi laughed and told him to be there at 4o'clock with some confirmed 'good news'.

Mandal smiled, but rather apprehensively.

After Piyush Mandal had left, Trivedi tried calling up Madan Oza but could not reach him. Oza had gone to his village, in Begusarai district. When Trivedi had called him at the time of leaving Ramgadh, he had said that he was enroute to his village to attend the funeral of his uncle. So Trivedi could not tell him to arrange for a call girl in Kolkata. He had taken Madan Oza services too much for granted but now he was so inconvenienced. Mandal did not seem to be the kind who could make such an arrangement. If he failed, Trivedi decided he would visit the red light area in Sonagachhi. He was very drunk but still desired a woman. But it was not possible to venture out alone and find one.

He was feeling sleepy and decided not to risk going out. He hung the breakfast card outside the door. The breakfast would be served at 8 am as per the hotel custom. That was the system at that hotel. The type of breakfast required and time is also noted and ticked on the card and put in knob outside the door. Sometime in the night the waiter will collect all such cards and deliver the cards to catering section. In the morning the breakfast will be served at the time indicated and menu as per requirement mentioned.

After breakfast the next day, Trivedi felt like going for a swim at the hotel pool to drive away his hangover from last night's whisky. When he reached the swimming pool, it wasn't very crowded. There were a few men swimming by themselves. There were seven or eight women at the ladies' side of the pool. They seemed to know each other and were enjoying as a group.

They could have belonged to the same family but did not resemble each other. Perhaps they might be office colleagues. The men however did not seem to know each other. They maintained the typical indifferent expression that was typical of five-star decorum and enjoying individually.

Trivedi enjoyed the sight of the young ladies swimming. It titillated him. When he tried to swim close by them, they swam to the other end. It seemed as if there was a mute understanding that one end of the pool was for ladies and the other was for men. Each group would swim up to the centre of the pool and turn back to their respective side from there. It was a vast pool. The Park Hotel was built during British India and was very spacious. After the swim, Trivedi had dried himself and wrapping a towel round himself, he had sat on one of the chairs. There was a young woman sitting a little distance from him.

He tried to make conversation by remarking that the pool water was quite cold that day.

She had only nodded.

Then he asked her if she was employed somewhere. She said they were all air hostesses.

"If you don't mind, can I say something?" He asked.

"Yes," she said.

"Your figure is very nice."

"Thank you," she said and abruptly got up to leave. She did not seem to have liked the comment.

In the afternoon Trivedi got back to his hotel room at 1.30 p.m. after having lunch with his friend. He had a long afternoon nap after that. At 4 o'clock, he called up Mandal. Mandal said he was on his way but reached the hotel at almost 5.00 p.m. Trivedi was eager to know if he had met the driver.

Mandal said he had met the driver and the driver was in fact waiting in the porch in his taxi.

Trivedi asked Mandal if he would like some coffee or whisky. Mandal said anything would do. Trivedi called for some whisky. Then he asked Mandal about the course of action. Mandal said they would have to book a room in another hotel.

Trivedi asked if it was a familiar hotel.

Mandal mentioned that he knew a hotel called Blue Moon near New Market. First they would reserve room there. Then the driver, Bansilal, would go and get a girl from College Street.

Trivedi said he did not want anyone from College Street.

"Then would you like one from Sonagachhi?"

"Yes, alright." Trivedi said.

Mandal thought that he would just get a call girl from somewhere. There was no way Trivedi would know. He would only have to coach the girl to say that she came from Sonagachhi.

Just then the waiter brought in the whisky and snacks and got signature of Trivedi on the hotel slip.

Mandal said the driver would get a girl from Sonagachhi.

Trivedi said he would go and select the girl himself.

"Oh my God! Sir, it is not safe. There were goons roaming the street and they might waylay you or loot you." Mandal warned.

Trivedi declared that he was not at all afraid. He was all charged up.

Mandal thought if Trivedi's intention was to go by himself to Sonagachhi and get a whore, why did he have to involve him in it? Mandal realized that Trivedi was an old hat at this game. He had used Mandal to get to a reliable hotel and for the sake of an escort in a strange place.

Mandal told him to reconsider going.

But Trivedi was adamant.

Mandal requested him to let him go to home, once a room had been booked at the hotel. He was afraid to stay there any longer.

Trivedi agreed." As you are afraid and don't wish to enjoy, there is no point in keeping you there. Alright, you can go once I am in the room."

"Shall we leave now?" Trivedi asked then.

"Let it get a bit darker, Sir. I have already spoken to the hotel. It will take just two minutes to book the room."

Trivedi ordered for some more whisky.

Mandal was quiet. Trivedi was doing all the talking. Trivedi told him, "Mandal, you can chat freely. You are now a friend. No need to be formal."

Mandal said, "Okay Sir."

The waiter brought in the whisky and took the required signatures on the tab bill from Trivedi.

After consuming three pegs, Mandal sheded his inhibition and asked Trivedi, "May I ask something, Sir?

"Yes."

"Sir, how do you manage all this in Ramgadh?" Mandal asked.

"Just like this. Someone always obliges." Trivedi told.

"Sir, don't mind it, but why don't you have a permanent mistress?" Asked Mandal.

"Wow, Good idea! Money is not a problem. Why don't you find one for me?" Said Trivedi.

"I can't do anything like that. I just made a casual suggestion." Said Mandal

"Agreed. I liked your idea. You know one lady officer in our company has kept a ricksha wala." Trivedi told.

"Oh God, what are you saying, Sir!" Mandal said.

"Yes, it is true. She is a senior Labour Welfare Officer, Kirti Patel is her name." Trivedi said

"What did you say is her name?" Mandal asked.

" Kirti Patel."

"Kirti has stooped to this level? She has really fallen on bad times." Mandal said.

"Do you know Kirti?" Trivedi asked.

"Yes Sir. I am sure she is the same Kirti who had loved me with all her heart. I had heard she was with RCL". Said Mandal with his voice trembling.

"So she is your first love, about whom you mentioned yesterday?"

Mandal was embarrassed. He felt he was the reason for her to be in such a state. He said, "Yes, Sir. I am feeling very bad about it"

He pleaded with Trivedi to keep his past affair with Kirti a secret, not to tell anyone, including Kirti. He had a solemn, emotional expression on his face and his eyes looked moist.

He added, "Sir, my family has been very unfair to her. So we had to suffer the consequences. My parents died in an accident. They had gone to my aunt in Asansol where their aurorickshaw met with an accident. My father died on the spot and my mother died four days later. But before closing her eyes forever, she said God had punished her for the injustice she had meted out to Kirti."

Trivedi got up and put a consoling hand on Mandal's shoulder.

Both were quiet for a while.

Then Trivedi remembered his mission, and remarked that the driver would be waiting for them. Mandal said, "Yes, sir. Let's go."

"Yes, let's finish the peg and leave."

"Sir, will you spend the whole night at that hotel or return to Park?" Asked Mandal.

Trivedi replied that he would return to Park hotel.

Mandal said "He would book the room at blue moon for some hours, but an extra day's payment would have to be made, if demanded by the hotel."

Trivedi had no problems with that.

After his mission accomplished, Trivedi returned to the Park Hotel at midnight; but not on his own feet. Driver Bansilal helped him up to his room. It was not a new scene for the Park Hotel staff; on rare occasions they did witness such scenes.

The waiter knocked at his door at 8.30 the next morning. There were three waiters holding trays laden with breakfast for three people. They laid the trays on the table. Trivedi asked who had ordered for so many. The waiters said there were breakfast cards hanging on his door so they assumed he had placed the order.

Trivedi protested that he had not hung those cards. The waiters said there were cards so they had brought breakfast for three at 8.30 AM. Trivedi had to sign the tab bill. Trivedi still felt the hangover of the previous night's whisky. He wanted some tea or coffee which was already in the tray. He freshened himself up and had a sandwich with his coffee. By then it was 9.15 a.m. The door bell rang again. Again the waiters brought in three breakfasts. He yelled at them to take it back. The waiters stacked the trays on the sofa saying that they had the order, as per breakfast cards placed. Trivedi had to sign the tab bill again. Trivedi sensed something wrong. He called up the manager and told him about it.

The Manager explained that every customer places the breakfast order with specifications about the time and type of breakfast preferred. It had been delivered according to the cards hanging on Trivedi's door from outside. These cards are collected at 5.00 AM. There was no bungling of any sort. Customers were instructed to do so at the time of checking-in.

Trivedi protested that why would he will order for so many breakfasts when he was the lone occupant. Besides, he had seen only two or three cards in his room.

The Manager had no clue. He said that they thought perhaps he had some guests over for breakfast. Sometimes customers would hold small office meetings on Sunday mornings in their hotel rooms.

Trivedi ended the call. He realized that someone was playing a prank on him. Someone had deliberately placed those cards on his door. All of a sudden, it occurred to him like a flash of light that it was perhaps the air hostesses who have done this.

They were getting their revenge for having stared at their bodies lustfully and for making lewd remarks about their nice figure. He again called the manager, "Shall I ask you something?"

"Yes, Sir. Sure."

"Have those air hostesses, who were staying in that wing, checked out of the hotel?"

"Let me check the register, Sir." He asked the receptionist to check. Trivedi held onto the phone. He asked if there were any more breakfast orders for his room.

The Manager replied that there were three more breakfasts ordered for his room at 10 a.m.

In an irritated tone Trivedi told him,"Please don't send up the trays, I will sign the tabs for them. This is just too much."

The Manager informed him that the air hostesses had left their rooms at early morning at 4.00 AM, perhaps they had to report for morning flights.

Trivedi could hear the receptionist laughing on the other end. "Thank you," he said and rammed the receiver down.

Trivedi wanted to have a bath but was in no mood to go to the swimming pool. His train was at 3.00 p.m. but he felt like checking out of that hotel immediately.

Colonel Sharma, Chief Vigilance Officer at RCL Headquarters, Ramgadh was sitting in his office. There wasn't any work in hand. It was about 4.00 p.m. Just then the phone rang. It was a call from the Chief Security Officer (CSO), Major Swami. He wanted to know if he could meet the CVO.

Colonel Sharma consented immediately.

Major Swami said he would be there in ten minutes. The Colonel said it was okay by him.

Colonel Sharma was recently transferred to RCL from Kolar Coalfields (KCL). Ramgadh was like homecoming for the Colonel because in the early part of his career as an officer, he had been posted at the Ramgadh Military Cantonment. He had joined as a bachelor, but had got married while he was in Ramgadh Cantonment. The memories of his newly married life were associated with Ramgadh. He had pleasant memories of the time he spent with his wife exploring the streets of Ranchi and Ramgadh. After Ramgadh, he got posted to Dibrugarh in Assam. At that time his wife was pregnant and he had left her at her mother's house and proceeded to Dibrugarh alone.

CSO Major Swami had been transferred to RCL from Satna Coalfields (SCL). He had served in the coalfields for six years now. Since both had a military background, they shared a good rapport with each other. They would meet often at the office or at their homes. Both preferred rum to whisky although whisky was never in short supply. They would meet often at each other's place over drinks. When some other officers joined them, they did not mind having whisky. Their wives too got along well with each other.

They never had to worry about their liquor because the military canteen was close by at Ramgadh cantonement and they could get their regular supply of bottles at subsidized rates.

Major Swami asked the secretary sitting outside the Colonel's office if he could go in. The secretary told him that the Colonel was waiting for him and had left instructions for Major Swami to be let in immediately.

"May I come in Sir?" Major Swami asked as he entered.

"Oh, that's not required,"said the Colonel as he shook hands with Major Swami and gestured him to take a seat.

The Colonel asked, "Any special reason for this visit?"

"Nothing special, just felt like making a visit. That's all."

"Very nice," said the Colonel.

They began to chat, but not about old times in the military service, but about RCL.

Major Swami told to Colonel "RCL was too much in the news. There were scandals about corruption and other issues. It is so surprising that the thefts committed by our Security personnel were detected by the local police. In fact the Managing Director sent for me. He put the newspaper in front of me and asked me to explain. I became a bit nervous. I promised him that I would root out the corruption in my department."

"Yes, you can surely do it," said the Colonel in an encouraging tone.

Major Swami requested the Colonel to help him in the task.

"Oh Yes, by all means," the Colonel assured him.

Then the Colonel told Major Swami about his meeting with the MD (Managing Director). The MD had also shown him the newspaper cuttings. The MD had said that the newspapers wanted sponsored advertisements and when we don't, they malign our company's name or threaten us with blackmailing tactics. They malign one officer or the other and try to extract money from us. Some low level reporters were using these methods. Such occurrences were on the rise in Jharkhand. It is through such newspapers that the management gets wind of the happenings in the coalfields. Generally no action is taken on these reports but it becomes necessary to take cognizance of such matters.

Major Swami listened quietly.

Then Colonel Sharma asked Major Swami if he knew what the Baniharee (impersonation) system was. He had not understood it fully and wanted the Major to explain it in detail.

Major Swami started to explain—In the years before coalmines were nationalized, it was a common practice to hire workers as substitute or casual labour. Only the regularized or permanent workers who wanted to go on leave could send a replacement worker in his place for that period.

Most of the permanent workers also used to work in their own fields. In the sowing season, they would go on leave. But the work of mining coal had to go on uninterrupted. They would therefore send temporary workmen in their place.

The practice of temporary or substitute labour continued even after nationalization of coalfields. But there was a rule that the casual or substitute workers must not work for more than 180 days or six months at a stretch. They would be dismissed before the end of 180 days because as per Labour Laws, if a worker worked for more than 180 days, he/she would have to be made permanent or regularised. The Baniharee system was a fall-out of this law. Everyone had a vested interest in this. Each link in the chain could get his share of the black money generated. The permanent workers had become less efficient and lazy. It was difficult to make them work by official standards. They misused the system to suit their greed and indolence. They continued with the practice of casual labour and would report on duty occasionally to prove their identity. Thus this impersonation system continued. There was not proper checking also, for namesake the checking was shown. The poor, casual workers slogged for a measly Rs150 or 200 per day and many times their 'owners' would pay even less keeping a balance amount with them, so that their impersonator should not fly away.

The owner even hired goons or musclemen to beat up the casual workers if they protested.

Colonel Sharma remarked that this was exploitation of the poor workers and it was necessary to set the system right by punitive action against the perpetrators. He further said that this was a serious socio-economical problem in our coalfields and should be tackelled on war footing. Let these slaved or bonded labour get freedom from misery and torture. They will definitely get some ulternate job with selfrespect.

Major Swami said it was difficult to stop this system because people from headquarters were also on the 'take'.

The officers from the Security and Vigilance department who conducted surprise raids were also beneficiaries of this corrupt system. Some of them were ever ready for inspection duty.

The peon came in with the coffee.

After the coffee break, Colonel Sharma said that the MD feels it was the responsibility of all officers to maintain the good image of the Company. Top echelons are unnecessarily subjected to questions from the Members of the Lok Sabha and Vidhan Sabha. The member of parliament from Gumla is now the Deputy Minister in Home Ministry at Delhi and he would frequently ask nuicent questions and give advice.

Major Swami said "As a military officer I too hate corruption but do not have the power to change the system."

Colonel Sharma said" The MD lends his full support to us in rooting out corruption; if not to root it out completely, we can at least work to bring it down. If we can constantly take steps to put fear in everyone's minds, corruption could be controlled."

Major Swami said that if they really had the MD's support in this, then the MD should openly declare his mission against corruption at the GM Coordination Meeting in the presence of all the General Managers. His message must reach all the officers, the managers, the engineers, the security officers and the sales officers.

Colonel Sharma said he would confer with the MD and on a specific assurance from him, they could take some concrete steps.

Major Swami nodded his head in agreement.

Colonel Sharma said, "Two heads are better than one', both of us together will be a formidable team. But we must decide beforehand which corrupt deals to tackle first and to what extent."

Major Swami agreed to this, "Yes, if the matter concerns very big names, we will have to be careful. We will suddenly start getting calls from higher –ups if we start probing such deals. Sometimes the Area GM and the Director also express their displeasure."

"I am going to submit a proposal to the MD after my talk with him. In that I am going to mention the need to curb corruption at the weigh bridge, at the Sales Depot and the impersonation (Baniharee) deployment. I am also going to suggest E-tendering for the purchases and civil work contracts. At present, general purchase and civil work is done on the basis of just three quotations received. Do you agree?" said Colonel.

"Yes, of course," the Major replied. Major Swami had already made the suggestion that the MD must declare his move against corruption to all the area GM's and the Department Heads at HQ as well. These Heads of Department must have the conviction that if need be, their officers will have to participate in the move. Especially the Heads of the Sales, Finance and Personnel Departments should be aware of this mission"

The Colonel appreciated Major Swami's plan and said, "Very good, you have thought in advance. Let us do something." He extended his hand for a warm handshake with the Major.

Major Swami had a bemused smile on his face when he left Col Sharma's office.

Renuka was scheduled to visit Maraal today. She also held the charge of DSP (Rural) and was expected to tour Ramgadh District as well. The constables at the various police stations were afraid of her. They would immediately report all important cases to her. The station-in-charge and the sub-Inspectors of the police station feared Renuka. After inspecting the police stations at Maraal and surrounding areas, she arrived at the RCL Office and headed straight for Kirti's chamber. She was familiar with it now.

Kirti was pleasantly surprised to see her. She took both her hands in a cordial welcome and seated her comfortably. Renuka said she was on an inspection visit to the police stations and felt like meeting Kirti.

Kirti asked her peon to fetch some cold water and some coffee.

They got down to chatting. Renuka asked if everything was peaceful at RCL.

Kirti replied that in a way, all was peaceful. There was always an undercurrent of hostility between the labour leaders and the management, and even a tiny spark would provoke it. As Welfare Officer, she would have a tough time pacifying the two parties.

Renuka commented that it was a good thing that she was a woman otherwise the labour leaders wouldn't have hesitated to beat her up.

Kirti agreed.

Renuka prepared to leave after the refreshments. Renuka requested her to stay for a while. Renuka asked her the reason. Kirti told her that it was nearing lunch time. Kirti was herself going to eat at the Guest House and she would have liked Renuka to lunch with her. She just had to call up the Guest House. Renuka hesitated a little but gave in when Kirti insisted on looking after her 'guest'. Renuka said she was not alone; there were two constables with her. Kirti assured her that it was not a problem at all.

Kirti called up the Guest House and informed them that she was arriving with the DSP in five to ten minutes. There was no hurry about lunch. She asked for the AC Suite number 2 to be kept ready.

Just then a labour leader stormed into the office. He looked very angry. He was taken aback to see Renuka in police uniform and thawed a little.

He said that there was a discrepancy in the allotment of quarters to the workers and he had come with an application.

Kirti asked him to hand over the application and told him that she would look into it later.

The man hurriedly put the application on her table and left.

Kirti and Renuka went to the Guest House in Renuka's jeep.

The caretaker had done up the suite and placed a vase of yellow roses on the table.

After making Renuka comfortable, Kirti went out and had a word with the caretaker. She told him to serve lunch to the two policemen at the dining table.

The caretaker informed her that it would take another half an hour for the lunch to be ready. Kirti said it was okay.

Back in the suite, Kirti asked Renuka if she would like to have a cold drink while the lunch was being prepared. Renuka declined as they just had had coffee in Kirti's chamber.

They resumed their chat. Kirti reminded her of the officer who was trying to court Renuka and asked what stage the affair had reached.

Renuka laughed. She said, "Nothing much. I haven't been very responsive. So things are moving very slowly."

"Better slow than not at all." Kirti said.

The topic veered to RCL. Kirti told her all about the coal thefts, Officers' liquor parties, and the Baniharee-labour leader nexus.

Renuka had heard of these matters but she got detailed information from Kirti.

Renuka was curious to know about the Baniharees so Kirti proceeded to give her the details. In conclusion she said that there seemed to be no remedy. People were so poverty-ridden that they accept these jobs to stave off starvation. They had to put aside their self-respect and dignity.

Renuka enquired if Kirti frequently had her lunch at the Guest House, whether she never cooked at home.

Kirti replied that she did not always eat at the Guest House; sometimes she ate there and sometimes at home.

Renuka asked her, "Who stays at home with you?"

Kirti asked her which home she meant; her house here or the one in Kolkata. Renuka said she meant the one at Ramgadh.

Kirti looked embarrassed. She looked thoughtful and nervous.

Renuka put her at ease with a disarming smile and said that she need not tell her if she didn't want to.

Kirti still looked grave but Renuka's disarming smile made her feel at ease. Kirti said that as they were now good friends, she would not keep any secrets from her.

Renuka prepared to listen.

Kirti told, "Well, Baldev lives with me."

Renuka looked at her in surprise. Now Kirti had no option than to reveal everything.

Kirti continued, "Let me tell you my entire life story. You seem to be at leisure today. It is not a very nice, happy story but I don't think I am doing any wrong in sharing it with you.

"Go ahead. I really am interested."

"I had a fun-filled college life. Piyush Mandal was my boy friend in those days. We loved each other; or rather, I was in love with him. I trusted him completely and he cheated me." Kirti started to tell her story.

Kirti went on to narrate how she had gone up to the friend's room and fallen victim to his lust. How she had got pregnant by him and how she was spurned by him and his family; the abortion she had to undergo. She talked about the bad name her neighbours had given her, and the impossibility of a marriage; and how she had taken up a job at RCL.

Renuka asked her if she had forgotten Piyush Mandal at all.

Kirti told her that it was not possible to forget one's first love. It is entrenched in our heart. It would annoy her many times but it had become an inseparable part of her life. Like a tender shower, it kept moistening her spirits. One has to admit that it is an insane love. One has to live with the memories and also try various means to forget it.

Kirti further said that life as such becomes the layers of curtains in the mind and heart. What you live normally and what disturbs you inside has to consealed. The flow of tears in loneliness has to be contained. You have to find the means to forget empliness of life.

Kirti felt overwhelmed with emotion. She was about to cry but controlled her tears. Renuka put her hand on Kirti's shoulder.

There was silence for a while.

"What happened after that?"

"After that?"

Renuka said, "What happened after you joined RCL?" She wanted to know how Baldev had entered Kirti's life.

Kirti had composed herself by then. "There were beasts at RCL too. I was young and beautiful then. Moreover I was staying alone. The men are men only, eyeing the lonely beautiful woman like me, but I was also cautious."

Renuka listened patiently. Kirti continued.

But I was helpless. I was used by one or two sexual maniacs. There was a Manager at Chhitarpur, where I had joined initially. He was fair and well-built.

His name was Balram Saluja. He belonged to Chandigadh. My body too succumbed to his lust. I was careful, though, to take birth-control pills. He would also use condoms. Our affair lasted three years. He fully enjoyed my body, played with it at will. In the beginning I wasn't very willing but later I started enjoying the sex myself. Then He got transferred. The new Manager was Sushant Banerjee. We would talk in Bengali. He was terrified of his wife so he would be tense while making love.

Some years passed. My brother found two marriage alliances for me from Kolkata. One of them rejected me on the grounds that I was very educated and employed. The other one rejected because they were expecting a huge dowry which we could not pay. My bothers did not try very hard to get me married because as long as my mother was alive, I would send money home every month for the upkeep of my mother. Their wives used to have a good time with the money I sent. I had made a mess of my life. I already had a bad name in Kolkata amongst my relatives. Some of our acquaintances had a part to play in giving me a bad name.

My state was like the miserable leaf that floated with the water current but could neither drown nor fly. The fate acomple was to be accepted by me.

"When did Baldev come into your life?'Renuka asked.

"Ten years ago. I used to go from Maraal to Ramgadh for stroll over there, or for a movie. While going, I used to go by bus or jeep. Baldev lived in Maraal. So he could afford to ply me home in his cycle-rickshaw in the evening. Any way he had to return to Maraal. I too felt comfortable travelling in a familiar rickshaw. Travelling in a jeep or a Trax with 15-20 other passengers made me feel very awkward. I would seek his cycle-rickshaw out at the rickshaw stand.

Those were the days when I was in a way, single, unattached. A new manager had taken charge. He was already been told nasty things about me and so he was ill-disposed towards me. His sole interest was money. He had no interest in sex. The Materials Manager was interested in me but lacked the courage. Very rarely did we have a fling, but I had to take the first step.

It was in such a state of mind that an incident occurred with Baldev. It was the rainy season. It wasn't raining when we started back from Ramgadh. Just after we crossed the Damodar river, it began to pour. Baldev was completely drenched, yet he paddled on. We came across a wayside tea -stall. I suggested that we have a cup of tea. There was an empty hut near the tea-stall. The tea-stall owner placed Moda (a small stool made of bamboo and rope) for me to sit on in the hut. I was also totally drenched in the rain which had lashed in on all sides of the cycle rickshaw. Baldev brought the tea cups. We sipped out tea. All the time he eyed my wet body. After we had our tea he abruptly got up and closed the door of the hut. It was raining heavily outside. I asked why he was closing the door. He came and held me close. I resisted. In the end I succumbed to his lust. Perhaps he had bribed the stall owner because no one had responded to my cries.

After all, the flesh has its own sensual craving! He brought me to an orgasm. He has plenty of stamina. He knows that when a woman is very satisfied, she holds her man tight, clings him. I don't know when my body cheated my mind and went out of control. He first caressed my breasts tenderly to rouse me. Then he kissed my thighs. First he was very tender with his foreplay, and when he sensed that I was totally roused, he became aggressive and demanding. I was very happy and satiated. When we reached Maraal, I called him into the house. We were still wet. We bolted the door and undressed. Once again we immersed ourselves in the act in the comfort of our bed. He paid frequent visits after that incident.

This is the fun of sex. What is suppressed in your mind surfaces again and again. The need of body is regular. I have read somewhere that primitive man had four important feelings and needs. They were "Bhay" "Nidra" "Bhook" and "Maithun". That is fear, sleep and appetite for stomach and sex. We all have evolved through generations and generations to civilized modern race. But still our primitive needs remain the same. If you fast even for a day and do not feed anything to your stomach with mind control, next day you are bound to eat, rather more than normal. Same is about sex. The body needs it and you can not go on fasting of it for a long. Rather it is a regular need. Whether you admit it or not. I am yet to read that Aacharya Rajnish book "Sambhog se Samadhi tak" sex to trance, but I will read it.

A few days later, I suggested that he should move in with me. His wife was pregnant at the time. I told him to take his wife's consent and shift in along with her. In any case, to satisfy his sexual appetite, he needed more than one woman. Baldev had been enjoying lot of women. Even after staying with me, he had affairs, which he had told me frankly.

For them, it was a big step moving from a shanty hut to a bungalow. Well, he shifted in and over a period of time, his children were born here. He has two daughters and a son. The older girl is nine years old and the boy is two. I am an aunt to his children. His wife calls me 'Didi" (elder sister).

"Didn't your society cavil at you? What was the reaction from your colleagues?" wondered Renuka.

My answer to them all is that if a man is allowed to have mistresses or a concubine, why should a woman not keep a man?

Why should society have double standards and allow men something that is taboo for women? Why should society view a man's moral transgressions differently from a woman's? I voiced my opinion very strongly. I have raised this question openly in front of many men and women. The men were without answers. They avoided the comments. They realized that this is the attack on their domination or male chauvinism. The ladies to whom, I have talked were of the opinion that I have to be afraid of society. What is customary for men can not be anyway ritual for woman. One or two women admitted that, I am correct, in pinpointing the difference in standards of society. Further they always advised me to get married anyhow. I never accepted their taunts meekly. In fact, it was a blessing in disguise, because other men stopped bothering me.

"Do you bear all the household expenses?" Renuka asked.

"I pay for the girls' school education, for the grocery, milk and other needs." Kirti told.

"Doesn't Baldev bear any expenses?" Renuka asked.

"He spends on vegetables and fruits. He feeds them well, gets them good clothes, and takes them to Ranchi or Ramgadh to the movies." Kirti told.

"You mean he goes on a spending spree?"

"No, not that much. I have opened a bank account for him. I have taught him about Fixed Deposits, recurring Deposits and so on. He also saves some money as I do. It seems he has booked a plot of land somewhere along Rajrappa Road, for which he says he has to pay in installments." Kirti informed.

"Looks like a happy domestic scene." Renuka remarked.

"Yes, domestic unit, without a real family for me." Kirti said, with a sting of sadness.

The caretaker served their lunch. Renuka noticed that Kirti had suddenly gone quiet. Perhaps she was feeling both relieved and awkward about laying bare the intimate details of her life like an open book.

Renuka said to her, "I have yet to see a courageous woman like you, who defies society, and doesn't care about the barbs aimed at her."

Kirti reciprocated by saying, "It is you who are truly fearless. You have carved an enviable place for yourself in this male-dominated police force."

Renuka smiled and a while later was on her way to Ramgadh.

Kirti was working at her desk late the next evening. She had to send some urgent documents to Headquarters the following morning. Her clerk was entering the data on the computer. She noticed that a mine worker was waiting at her door. She could not recognize him as he was covered with coal dust. Her clerk told her that the worker wanted to meet her. She told the clerk to let him in.

The worker went around the table and touched her feet and greeted her politely.

"Who are you?"

"I am Jaggu Manjhi, Baniharee of Ramnaresh. I have come to you for help." He spoke in Bangala language as he knew that Kirti could speak the language.

Kirti recognized him vaguely as the man who was beaten up badly by Ramnaresh after the vigilance raid.

She asked irritably, "What is it?"

Jaggu was silent for a moment.

Kirti urged him to speak.

"I have come to beg your favour."

"What do you want? Speak up."

"Please take me off this Baniharee bondage." Jaggu requested earnestly.

"What do you mean?" Kirti asked.

"Please put me on another job. I can work as casual labour or daily wage worker anywhere in the mine premises with your blessings. Or, send me to a civil or building contractor." He told.

He gave a pitiful entreating look.

"Have you quarelled with Ramnaresh?" She asked.

"No, nothing like that". He replied.

"Then what is it?"

"I am constantly in fear of him. He has a big knife on him always. He always has his musclemen around him who are ever ready to beat me with their stick. He never pays me my full wages. If I am absent for one day, he cuts two days' wages. If I protest, he beats me up." Jaggu told her his pitiable state of affairs.

Jaggu's eyes filled up with tears.

Kirti became pensive. She tried to explain to him that the authority to hire someone was with the PO, Mr. Sinha and he appoints only those people who are recommended by the Manager, Prabhunath Singh. You have no education. Moreover, you are Ramnaresh's man. If we hire you, Ramnaresh will create a hue and cry.

"Let him shout."

"How can you say that? You see, he supplies milk, curds and ghee free of cost to the officials here. Plus, a portion of your Baniharee wages also reaches each one of them every month. Actually I should not be telling you all this; but you seem to be a simple, poor man who has come from some remote village in BengaI. I feel pity for you and so I have told you the truth." Kirti said.

Jaggu fell at her feet and begged her to do something.

Kirti told him that it was going to be difficult. She would still try to talk to the Manager but it might cost some money.

Jaggu asked her if he should meet Prabhunath Singh. Kirti said, "Wait until I tell you. And meet him alone."

He expressed his gratitude and once again stepped forward to touch her feet. But she stopped him and told him to leave. He went out joining his palms in gratitude.

Jaggu rues his fate. He felt like a man without roots who neither belonged to Kundapara in Birbhaum nor to Maraal in Jharkhand. His life was like a burden of coal basket on his head. One feels the weight of the basket on one's shoulder when you carry it; but even when you don't, you still feel your shoulders burdened with that weight. There is a lot of burden of responsibilities, like the burden of his untended land in Kundapara, the money for his mother, Radha's plight and most of all the burden of his debt.

These heavy loads he was constantly bearing on his shoulders. He had migrated from Kundapara in the hope of earning some decent money, to have enough to eat, but it did not happen like that. Several times both he and Radha had prayed to goddess Kalimata for succour, but their fate did not change. He often visited the temple; the priest took money from him for the pooja and blessed him that the goddess would drive away all his troubles. But his misery still remained the same. There seemed to be no hope.

A fortnight passed. Jaggu felt that perhaps Kirti would have spoken to the Manager by then. That day, the Loading Supervisor, Ashok Kumar Jha was on leave. Prabhunath Singh and the Sales

Manager, Deepak Chatterjee had come to check that things were running smoothly, at coal loading point.

Deepak Chatterjee had to leave on summons from Sinha. The weigh bridge clerk sent Jaggu to fetch tea. Jaggu brought the tea. For a brief moment, just he and Prabhunath Singh were in the office. The clerk had gone out. He assumed that Kirti must have spoken about him to the manager and it seemed too good an opportunity to resist. So he said to Prabhunath, "Sir, I have a humble request."

Prabhunath snapped at him, "What is it?"

"Sir, give me a chance to serve at your feet."

"Speak clearly."

"Please take me on as a casual labour or some other job."

"Hey, you are a Baniharee for Ramnaresh. Why do you need another job?" Asked Prabhunath Singh angrily.

"Sir, please do me this favour. Kirti Madam must have told you."

The last sentence uttered by Jaggu incensed Prabhunath. He bellowed, "Who is she to tell me? You get out of here."

Jaggu stood there, his hands joined.

"Did I not tell you to get out?"

The clerk heard the loud voice and came running. Jaggu quietly walked out.

Prabhunath ranted and raved, "These idiots want jobs. They don't have an iota of brains. And of all people, Kirti was going to recommend whom should I hire!"

The clerk did not utter a word. Prabhunath walked out of the office in a huff, leaving the rest of his tea untouched, and drove away in his jeep.

Jaggu realized that he should have first asked Kirti Madam whether she had spoken to Prabhunath Singh. He had behaved impulsively and lost all his chances of a job.

The next day he went to Kirti Madam's office to meet her, but she was away at Ichotu Area Office.

On the third day, he met her in the office and narrated the incident concerning Prabhunath Singh. Kirti reprimanded him, "Why did you have to speak out of turn? Did I not tell you not to approach until I tell you to do so? Don't you know his nature? You have seen him for so many years now."

Jaggu kept apologizing. She did not respond. She gestured him to go away.

Loading Supervisor Ashok Kumar Jha was back on duty after four days.

Ramnaresh presented himself at his office on Saturday, after the wagon had been loaded with coal. He had two of his musclemen with him. They caught hold of Jaggu and began to thrash him. He asked, "What have I done?"

Ramnaresh said, "You want another job, isn't it? Here it is." And they began to give him blows with their sticks and walked out. Prabhunath had told Ashok Kumar and Ashok Kumar had conveyed it to Ramnaresh.

Jaggu somehow managed to reach his humble hut. Radha could make out from a distance that he had been beaten up. She ran up to him and helped him into the hut. His whole body had taken the beating and his face was swollen. Radha began to abuse Ramnaresh. She invoked curses upon him. "May that wicked man be destroyed? May he die hungry! May all his family suffer and starve and get beaten up!"

She warmed up some mustard oil on the earthen stove and spread an old sheet on the cot and asked Jaggu to lie down and she tended to his bruises with the warm oil. He groaned in pain. All that suffering made her cry. Jaggu was also in tears. In fact he felt like sobbing uncontrollably. Radha told him to have it all out and not to suppress it. He rested his head on her shoulder and wept. He looked into her eyes. They felt that both of them were caught in a vortex of despair and misfortune. It took quite a while for them to calm down. She got up to cook. He continued to lie down; his body and mind were in pain. He felt he was destined to suffer his helpless miserable existence of a poor man and so was Radha along with him.

Jaggu saw his life like a boat without a boatman; the boat floated wherever the current of water took it. Even if he was the boatman, he could not work the oars or the oars would not reach the water. The water continues to flow turbulently, and the boat tosses along without any direction. He remembered how he loved boating in his childhood, to row the oars with his father. He was his father's favourite, his brothers were jealous of him. They still grudged against him. It had been a small river in which he rowed his boat. Now he was rowing his life's boat in the mighty Damodar river. The river in flood that broke its banks, and flowed unchecked, unrestrained, uprooting the tiny huts and trees along the banks!

He wondered how much more he had to suffer. He doubted whether he could ever make this degenerated and wandering stream of life reach a safe bank. Perhaps he would drown in a whirlpool. What would become of Radha? She was his pillar of strength that is how he has endured this far. Her tears drop on his back and his love for her gushes forth. Why she had to come in my ill-fated life? He should have been alone. He remembered how she came into his life as a ten or eleven year old child- bride. But even then she had been so sensible. She had never complained or thrown any tantrum about anything. She had accepted his fate as her own. He could feel the sobs rising within him at these thoughts.

The next day was a Sunday. He rested the whole day. He did not have the energy to go for work on Monday either. But Naval Prasad and Suresh Singh, the two musclemen of Ramnaresh were at his door and dragged him to work. He felt too weak to work but he had to toil. Ramlal lent him a helping hand. He kept telling Ramlal not to bother. Ramlal was very angry with Ramnaresh but did not have the courage to do anything. He knew Ramnaresh wouldn't hesitate to beat him too. Besides, he knew that his wife, Janaki, and daughter-in-law Parbati would admonish him for getting involved unnecessarily.

Two days passed in this miserable state. Radha would give him an oil massage every day. He somehow managed to put in the day's labour. One of the workers had returned from a visit to Kundapara, Jaggu's village. He brought the news that Jaggu's mother was unwell. Jaggu wished to go and meet her but there was no way he could seek Ramnaresh's permission. Besides, he would need an advance payment, which was impossible to get. He could borrow some money from Ramlal, but that would not be enough.

Jaggu then approached some of Ramnaresh's friends. They first ticked him off. Janu Prasad was slightly better than the rest. He conveyed the matter to Ramnaresh. At first Ramnaresh didn't budge. Then he said he would think about it. Janu Prasad then told Jaggu to fall at Ramnaresh's feet and beseech him.

Three days passed. Jaggu got a telegram about his mother's death. He felt numb. He thought only a mother loved selflessly, the brothers were selfish and insincere.

Jaggu went to Ramnaresh's house with the telegram and falling at his feet, began to cry. He begged him to lend him some money and let him go. Ramnaresh brushed him off. Jaggu didn't budge. He continued to sit there. Ramnaresh told him to borrow from the moneylender. Jaggu told him that he hadn't repaid the earlier debt how could he borrow some more?

Finally Ramnaresh's wife took pity on Jaggu. At her behest Ramnaresh gave him the fare and Rs.1500 for expenses, a total of Rs.2500/-.

Jaggu obsequiously fell at his feet to thank him. Ramnaresh warned him that he must return to Maraal and not stay put in Birbhaum. He had to return and repay the debt. Otherwise Ramnaresh would come to Birbhaum and make him pay twice the amount.

Jaggu returned to his hut, a sad man. Radha had gone to wash utensils at some household. Jaggu sent a woman neighbour to call her. On her way home, Radha chanced upon Ramnaresh's wife. She gave her five hundred rupees and said she should have some money on a journey like this. When Radha fell at her feet in gratitude, she told her that it is not charity. Radha should return it from the wages she earned for washing and cleaning job.

Radha nodded.

Ramlal and Parbati paid Jaggu a visit when they heard about the telegram. Jaggu embraced Ramlal and cried; Radha found solace in speaking her heart out to Parbati.

Jaggu reached his village Kundapara, near Birbhaum, the following evening. He felt very grieved that he could not meet his mother on her death bed. He expressed his feelings to his brothers. His elder brother told him that he had sent a word to Jaggu about her illness, but Jaggu had not come. Jaggu slapped himself. His older sister-in-law consoled him saying that Maaji (mother) was no more, there was no point in feeling bad now.

The middle brother Keshu didn't speak much. He and Jaggu had fought over something in the past.

The custom was to collect the ashes the next day. Jaggu's mother's ashes had been piled under a tree a little distance away from the place of cremation because another dead body had to be cremated at the same spot the next day. Since the cremation took place on the river bank, it wasn't a problem to immerse the ashes and bones in the river. Jaggu asked for two or three bones (ashthi) so that he could immerse them in the waters of the Damodar river.

"Where will you keep them till then?" Keshu queried.

"I won't keep them in the house. I will keep it in an earthen pot and bury it in a corner of a hut in the field. I will take the pot with me when I go." Jaggu replied.

The elder brother agreed to this and so did his maternal uncle. (Mama) The Mama said it was a good idea as they were unable to immerse the remains in the holy Ganga. Keshu had to agree quietly.

The next day the elder brother asked Jaggu if he had brought any money as they had to feed the villagers on the thirteenth day as per ritual. Jaggu gave him rupees fifteen hundred. Keshu shouted angrily, "How will this suffice?" Jaggu told him that his boss had given him only that much amount.

Keshu walked out in a huff.

The elder brother however said it was alright. He would borrow some money and when Jaggu goes back he could send the same towards repayment.

Jaggu had no choice but to nod his head in agreement. That day the maternal uncle was not in the house. He had gone to his village nearby.

On the thirteenth day ritual, half the village was fed a meal of fish and rice and dessert (rasgulla). Every one ate well. The following day all the expenses incurred on their mother's death were calculated. The brothers burdened, Jaggu with a demand of another two thousand rupees. They told him to send the amount as soon as possible from Maraal.

In the end the topic of division of the farmland was brought up. The elder brother said the division would be done in the presence of some villagers. He had asked the maternal uncle and his wife to stay back for the talks. This aunt (Maami) was a distant relative of Keshu's wife so for most of the time she sat next to Keshu's wife.

That day Radha had a fever. She had been made to toil hard with the chores for the past few days. At night she advised Jaggu to discuss not just about the division of the farm land but also their rightful share in the house. Jaggu explained that the other brothers had already claimed their rights and were living in it for so many years. Radha told him that despite all that he should demand possession of at least one room. The mother's room was vacant now and they could ask for that and keep it locked. Jaggu said the brothers would refuse as they wanted to use that room to store the cattle feed and farm equipment in that room. She was not convinced. She argued that they could keep all the equipment in the corner of the cowshed as before. When they returned home for good in the future, they would need a room for themselves.

Jaggu did not say a word. The next morning he called for a village doctor. He gave Radha some medicine for her fever and asked her to rest.

This did not go well with the middle sister-in-law. She started grumbling about Radha's rest. Poor Radha got up from her bed and offered to do whatever she could.

The farmland was apportioned in the presence of the village elders. The two brothers had already taken their father's share of the land. They had taken four acres each. The remaining three acres which were on his mother's name were to come to Jaggu. This piece of land was barren but was near the river. In the rainy season, the floods would wash out the harvest. Only if the river was not in flood, the land would give a good yield because of the silt deposited during the previous flood.

Jaggu declared that he would not go back to Jharkhand. He would stay in Kundapara and tend the land. The brothers vetoed this idea. They told him that the returns from the land would not be enough.

Even they had to work elsewhere during the non-agricultural season. Jaggu should continue to work in Jharkhand and send some money when the need was felt. Jaggu did not know that the real reason was that this piece of land had already been mortgaged by the brothers by taking their mother's thumb impression on the deed.

Jaggu too was not very keen on staying in Kundapara mainly because his brother Keshu looked at Radha with sexual desire. Keshu's wife Sonu was dark and fat. And he lusted for the lissome Radha. An incident had occurred four years ago. Radha was in the early stage of her pregnancy at the time. Keshu tried to molest her even in that state. When she was just returning from her bath from the backyard, he had put his arms around her. She managed to extricate herself from his grasp. He had warned her not to talk about it to anyone. In the evening, after returning from the fields, Keshu and Jaggu got into a fight. Sonu blamed Radha. Keshu had lied to her and she called Radha a flirtatious woman of loose character. Jaggu slapped Keshu hard and was about to slap Sonu but Radha intervened. Their mother came shouting but Sonu had pinned Radha down on the floor and was pummeling her stomach. Their elder brother and his wife were away at the time, attending her nephew's christening ceremony.

Radha had to rush to the bathroom. She was bleeding profusely. First the village medic was consulted, then a doctor. Her baby had died inside. Radha was deeply shocked and dejected. She behaved like a lunatic for some days. She would wail, "My son, my son!" And then she would hold Jaggu close and weep. It was during this time that one of Jaggu's friends had come to Kundapara on leave. He worked for a civil contractor at Ramgadh. He promised to find Jaggu a job so Jaggu had come to Maraal.

At Ramgadh, when they consulted another doctor, they were told that Radha's uterus had been injured and it was difficult for her to bear a child again. Jaggu realized that back home in Kundapara, there was only one hungry wolf in the form of his brother Keshu, but here in Maraal there were so many of them ready to pounce. A poor man's wife is always addressed as Bhabi (Sister-in-law) but a rich man's wife is Didi (Elder sister). A beautiful woman like Radha is always a focus of attraction. Once, Radha thrashed a lascivious man. He was thrashed first by Radha and then by Jaggu. Since then everyone kept an arm's distance from her. But there is never any dearth of lewd and lecherous men.

Radha's claim to her mother-in-law's room was honoured but it was only a formality. The elder brother said that only when Jaggu came home he could use it, at other times it would be used as a store room for the farming equipment. Jaggu was left with no choice but to agree with the terms.

Radha's fever came down in a couple of days. The village medic prescribed some medicines. Jaggu and Radha took the road back to Ramgadh.

Jaggu felt sad about leaving Kundapara. He did not want to leave it. But there would no longer be his mother's loving care. Besides, he would need a lot of money to buy the seed, fertilizers, equipment and cattle to tend his land. It was difficult to find daily wage jobs in the area. There were no factories or mines in the area, only agricultural activities. Finding a roof above their heads in

Kolkata was impossible. In Maraal at least one could put up a shanty anywhere. If they were ousted from there, they could put it up elsewhere. Besides, there were many others who lived in huts like him and whenever there was an anti-encroachment drive, all the dwellers would unite.

Jaggu's plan was to pay up the money-lender's debt first. Then he could say good-bye to the bastard Ramnaresh and find another job in far away Chhittarpur or Gola. On their train journey back, Radha too was dejected and sad. She had not been able to visit her parents' home at all. Her brother and his wife had attended the thirteenth day ceremony of her dead mother-in-law. They had not shown any warmth or eagerness to invite her home. After all the affairs had been attended to, Jaggu was in a hurry to get back to Ramgadh. On the train, Radha mentioned that they should have stayed back at Kundapara. Jaggu asked her, "Where would we find work? What will we eat? What can we get out of just three acres of land? Where do we get the money to invest in sowing?"

Radha told him that she did not feel like returning to Maraal. She had some uncanny fear about going back. That bastard Ramnaresh would keep beating Jaggu and every blow he took was like a blow on her body. There has to be a limit to the tears and misery of the poor.

Jaggu agreed with her. "True. For the poor people like us, life is just about moving from the frying pan into the fire. Two grains of rice for the pot and two to sow. A hand-to-mouth existence! I feel guilty that I cannot keep you in comfort. You could eat fish to your heart's content at the thirteenth day ritual lunch. It was a sad occasion alright. But at other times I can never buy you such a large quantity of fish. We cannot always afford to eat to our heart's content. I know you relish fish. But I can rarely get enough for you."

Radha urged him not to be so disgruntled. Maybe there were better days ahead!

Jaggu responded half-heartedly, "Goddess Kali alone knows!"

Five Years Later

July 2005

Jaggu was loading coal into the truck. He was now working for a new master, Sardarji Joginder Singh. Joginder was a decent man. He would pay Jaggu his weekly wages properly. Now Jaggu's financial problems had eased a little. His debt had reduced to half. He had started loading coal onto the trucks in the morning. By evening, he and four other co-workers were loading a fourth truck. The co-workers were exhausted. One of them suggested that they would do the rest of the loading the next day.

Jaggu said he would ask the Sardarji first.

Sardarji realized that the workers were very tired. He gave Jaggu a hundred rupee note and told him to buy some refreshments for the team of workers. If they felt like it, he was ready to offer them a peg of liquor each. He had a bottle with him.

Jaggu conveyed this to his group. The men were thrilled. One of them approached Sardarji and fetched half a bottle; about 375ml. Jaggu did not wish to drink. He contented himself with snacks (samosa, pakora) and a cup of tea.

The Sardarji had convinced the new Loading Supervisor, Sumant Singh to continue with the loading even in the darkness, past 6.00p.m. Ashok Kumar Jha the previous supervisor, has been transferred out and Deepak Chatterjee, the Sales Manager was also persuaded to let the loading continue past 6.00p.m. Thus there was no problem at all. This arrangement was possible with increased bribe only.

The truck was loaded very quickly by the team of workers. They were all very motivated and ready to load one more truck. The Sardarji covered the coal-laden truck neatly with a tarpaulin and asked the workers to leave. The workers departed bidding good-bye to the Sardarji. Jaggu was instructed by the Sardarji to report for loading early the next morning and to get his team of workers too.

Jaggu nodded his head. On the way back home, he went to a grocer's shop and purchased some oil. The grocer lent him a bottle for the oil, which Jaggu would have to return later. He bought enough vegetables like onions, potatoes to last for a couple of days. When he reached his hut, He washed his hands and feet with the water stored in a drum at the entrance of his house. The door was closed. There was a small lock on the door. He opened it and entered the dark hut. He looked at the darkness desultorily. He felt like this every evening. He hated entering his hut in the evening. He took out a match box and looked for the lantern. He pulled up its wick and lit it. In the dim light, he felt this even more empty and unwelcome. He stood there for a couple of minutes and then changed his clothes and lied down on the simple bed. After lying down for ten-fifteen minutes, he felt the hunger pang in his stomach. He thought he must put some food into his stomach. The samosa he had eaten made him feel somewhat full. But then he would have to get up late at night feeling hungry. He lit the stove, took some water from the earthen pot and washed the rice grains. He put them in a vessel to cook and again lied down on his bed while the rice was getting cooked.

He emptied the vegetable bag, picked and cleaned the vegetables, sorted the coriander and the spinach. He went out to throw the discarded stalks. He put the vegetables in a basket. The rice was ready by now. There was a left-over vegetable curry from the morning's cooking. He warmed the curry and served himself a plate of rice and curry. He blended the rice and curry with his fingers and put a morsel in his mouth. He choked over this, perhaps he had put too much chilly in it. The first morsel reminded him of Radha. Tears streamed down his eyes. Before taking his second morsel, he looked around the hut. A hut without Radha, a lonely hut!

He remembered how her very presence would make the drab, listless hut come alive. The normally solemn looking Radha would laugh merrily when Jaggu was around. She would look so perfectly happy. She would lovingly tend to his wounds but now she was no more. Who was going to heal his emotional wounds? The second morsel was still in his hand. He forced it into his mouth. Then he drowned it with a gulp of water. He steeled himself and began to eat from the plate in his hand.

After his meal, he came out and scrubbed the utensils. He could see the lights in the distance. Everything looked obscure. But he was used to it. Tomorrow he would have to go to the bank of the Damodar and fetch some water. He would have to get up early for that.

He shook the dust off his mattress. He pulled a thin sheet over his face and lay down. His body felt tired and was in need of rest. But his mind was overcome with grief. He began to cry. He wiped the tears with the corner of his sheet. This loneliness was eating at the very core of his heart, always tormenting and shocking. Tears trickled down his cheeks. The night wore on. He felt a kind of stupor but his mind found no rest. He remembered Radha's beautiful face, her dainty mannerisms, he tossed and turned in his bed. He remembered again and again and felt a deep remorse that such a sensible, understanding and caring woman had come into his life and then gone away so tragically. He sobbed and sobbed and somewhere between his sobs, he fell asleep. Another dark night had merged into his world of eternal darkness. The Sun would rise and set on another sorrowful day for Jaggu.

Renuka's work load increased towards the evening. The Chief Minister of Jharkhand state was expected to tour the area in a couple of days. There had to be foolproof security and traffic arrangements. Renuka had to coordinate with the various departments. It was 7.30 p.m., while she dealt with all this. She came back to her bungalow in her jeep.

Little Aradhya came scampering out the moment she heard the jeep. Renuka picked her up in her arms.

Aradhya announced, "Papa is at home."

"Is that so?"

"Yes. We were playing ball", said Aradhya.

Renuka walked towards the porch and put Aradhya down. She sat on a chair and took off her shoes. She left her socks in the shoes. She entered the house and noticed Kripal Singh in the kitchen. Renuka had a wash; she wiped her hands and sat on the sofa. Aradhya seated herself on Renuka's lap. By then Kripal Singh had come into the drawing room with two cups of coffee set on a tray. He took out a bottle of cold water from the refrigerator and offered it to Renuka. She said, "Thank you." He replied, "Welcome." They smiled at each other.

Renuka called out, "Buaji, (Kripal Singhs' aunt— Father's sister) come and join us for coffee!" Buaji came out with a cup of coffee. She also had a glass of Bournvita for Aradhya. She again went into the kitchen to fetch a plate of biscuits and placed it on the center table. Aradhya quickly picked up two cream biscuits and gave one to her father. Kripal Singh gave her a peck on the cheek. Renuka told her to finish off the glass of Bournvita.

Kripal Singh asked, "You had to make arrangements for the Chief Minister's visit, didn't you?"

"Yes. But how did you come so early?"

Kripal Singh told her that he had put all the responsibility on the Deputy Collector's shoulders. Perhaps he had spoken to Renuka about it.

"Yes, he did. He talks with exaggerated respect."

"You are the SP and also his Boss' wife. Naturally he is respectful towards you!" Kripal Singh said.

Aradhya picked up two more cream biscuits and offered one to Renuka. Renuka asked if she had finished her Bournvita. Aradhya showed her the cup, it was almost empty.

Renuka went into the bedroom and changed into her night gown. She had put on weight. Kripal Singh looked at her. Buaji understood the expression in their eyes and hurried towards the kitchen. Renuka asked her, when she was on the way to kitchen, what vegetable was cooked for dinner. Buaji told her she had made ridgegaurd *(ninwa)* curry for Babua (Kripal Singh's pet name). "Ninwa, what in your parts is called *turai* (Ridge Gourd) or *tel dodka* and for you I have fried dry potato."

Aradhya demanded that the cartoon channel on TV be switched on. Kripal Singh told her to let Mamma watch the news channel. By then Renuka had surfed the headlines. She told Kripal Singh to put on the cartoon network for Aradhya.

Renuka went closer to Kripal Singh and whisperd in his ear, "Why did you look at me like that when I came out in my nightgown?"

"Just like that, casually."

"What do you mean by that?"asked Renuka.

"I was looking at your figure. Your post-natal confinement has filled you out, you look plump." Said Kripal Singh.

"I must increase my Sunday Drill workout. I must get back in shape." She said

"Oh you look marvelous and gorgeous the way you are now." He said.

"That's being really naughty!" She said accusing his mischievousness.

They looked at each other. Just then the phone tinkled. It was Kripal Singh's friend on the line.

"What does Avdhesh Singh has to say?" Renuka asked Kripal Singh after he had put down the receiver.

"There is some talk about my transfer either to Deoghar or to Dhanbad."

"Didn't you ask him if there was any news about my transfer?" Asked Renuka.

"The orders are on hold for that, he said," said Kirpal.

"What does it mean?"

Kripal Singh explained that according to the Government Rule, both I and you must be posted to the same station. So the General Administrative Department has to talk to your IG and the Home Ministry. There might be some delay in our transfer. It could be that other officers might get their transfer orders before mine; then adjusting our transfers to the same place might be a difficult proposition.

Renuka asked him, "Why are you in such a hurry?"

"I am trying to avoid a posting to a Naxalite (terrorist) area. It might not be safe there with Aradhya. I am making efforts to not go there."

Renuka said "but—".

He cut her off mid-sentence saying, "Look, our posting is a certainty. Why should we not try to get a posting to a place of our choice?"

Renuka said it was alright.

"I think our transfer will not take place so soon. Only when some officer makes a blunder somewhere or some officer is posted out under political pressure, will there be a chance of our transfer."

Renuka said, "Let's wait and watch."

Both were lost in their own thoughts, saying nothing for a while. Buaji announced that dinner was ready. Kripal, Renuka, Aradhya and Buaji sat at the dining table. Aradhya sat in Kripal Singh's lap being fed by mom. Buaji smiled with contentment at the happy threesome.

At Ramgadh, Madan Oza was sitting in the coal yard. He was a worried man these days. The police were keeping a strict eye on his illegal coal trade. He had to tread very carefully in his business. In the last year's general elections, the government at the Jharkhand state got changed. It was a different political party, new contacts were under way. He had spent huge amounts of money on building up a network of 'connections' with politicians from previous government, but all these were of no use now. Still they had to be maintained because one never knew if the same people got elected again in the next general elections.

The main issue was that the police protection he enjoyed all these years had vanished. He still managed a little police support at Ranchi, but in Ramgadh it was impossible. He had been arrested once but had managed to get bail by spending a lot of money on lawyers and in courts. Madan Oza was shaken up after this incident.

Madan Oza had called Naval Prasad to meet him with a report about the work in the last eight days. In the meeting, Naval Prasad was giving a complete report about the truck loading work—the number of trucks loaded, the number of loaders hired, how many were yet to be loaded and so on. Naval Prasad also wanted some advance for disbursement of wages. Some of the trucks were owned by Madan Oza; and for several other trucks he would collect the rentals directly. So Naval Prasad always had to face a cash crunch due to untimely settlement of loading of Madan Oza's trucks and had no choice but to take an advance on account of this.

Madan Oza asked Naval Prasad about Ramnaresh and whether anybody had gone to Hazaribaug to meet him. Naval Prasad told him that Suresh Singh had been sent to meet Ramnaresh in the jail, but he was not allowed to meet him on the grounds that Suresh Singh had come after the specified no. of visitors met Ramnaresh already. No more nos were entiteled. Some relatives from Ramnaresh's home town had been allowed to meet him, he had heard.

Naval Prasad continued with his information, "Suresh Singh then told the jail staff that he wanted to meet Bhauji (Ramnaresh's wife). It was in the entiteled no. of visitors and he was sent to the other side of the jail, the female ward. There again there was some formality of visiting register entry and he was allowed to meet her.

Madan Oza asked, "And how is she?"

"Suresh Singh says she has lost a lot of weight and looks very thin. For someone who is used to a diet of milk, curd and butter, dry jail food is going to take its toll, naturally."

"Oh God, I really pity Bhauji!" said Madan

"It is a good thing that only two years are balance of her sentence, she will be released after that. But Boss Ramnaresh and his brothers-in-law (wife's brothers) will have to toil in jail for six more years. Wonder what condition they will be in at the end of their jail term!" Said Naval.

Madan Oza appreciated the loyalty of Suresh Singh and Naval Prasad towards Ramnaresh. They were patiently waiting for their master to come out of jail. He knew Ramnaresh would hardly have any money left by the time he finished his jail sentence, what with all the expenses on lawyers and courts. Madan thought, that bastard SP refused to take a bribe! Had she been pliable, even if money had to be spent, Ramnaresh would have had at least a reduced sentence or been acquitted.

Madan Oza also had to go through a lot of mental torture in Ramnaresh's case. It was Madan's strict principle that once he put his hand into something, he would not rest until the task was done. Madan was an adept in achieving success in a task, in whatsoever way. But in Ramnaresh's case; he faced failure as there were too many complications

Madan Oza was particularly angry with Renuka. None of his tricks he applied so far had worked with her. He tried to have her transferred, but he failed. Just when there seemed to be some hope of dealing with the matter successfully, there was a change in the government. It had now become impossible to harass or assault Renuka. She herself had been very cautious. Her network of spies or informers would tip her off about any plans against her. Besides, her husband was the Collector, so she wielded a lot of power. Kripal Singh also was a changed man after his marriage with Renuka. He no longer paid any heed to Madan Oza.

Madan Oza had been able to sustain as he had a lot of political connections. Although now his illegal businesses were drastically restricted, he was still carrying on with them quietly. Renuka had driven him to desperation but was not able to throw him out. This was his only consolation. He knew Renuka had a watchful eye on him, so he too was very careful and alert.

"How should we deal with Jaggu Manjhi?" Naval Prasad wanted to know.

"What do you mean?" Madan Oza countered.

"Last time you had mentioned that Jaggu must be done away with." Said Naval Prasad.

Madan replied, "I think we will have to wait for some time. Let that Sardarji for whom he is working, leave Maraal. And let that bitch SP woman be transferred out first. It will be a big risk if we do it now."

Naval Prasad looked at Madan. The lion had turned into a lamb now!

Deepak Chatterjee, the Sales Manager at Maraal arrived at the RCL Headquarters in Ramgadh on official business. He had learned that the Satish Trivedi, General Manager, Sales, had taken ill and was hospitalized. It was fifteen days since the Deputy GM, Uttam Singh, had taken charge.

It has been nearly three months since Uttam Singh was transferred to RCL. Deepak was not yet well acquainted with him. But Uttam Singh seemed like a past master at his 'work'. He had unabashedly asked Deepak, about the 'extra income'. Deepak had brought the cash but it was meant for Trivedi's pocket. So he had promised Uttam Singh that he would get the money for him later. A part of the cash that Deepak had brought included the cut from Baniharee wages also. Prabhunath Singh and Sumant Singh would give Deepak Chatterjee some amount every month. Some years ago, Ramnaresh and others would give the Baniharee's share directly. But now as they had lost their jobs, other loaders had replaced them and they hired new Baniharees under them.

In those days, Colonel Sharma, very strict and upright CVO had taken charge. He had conducted raid after raid relentlessly. He had the support of the security, for a change.

Jaggu Manjhi, Kali Manjhi and others had been caught in one of these raids. Ramnaresh and his two close cronies, Janu Prasad and Ayodhya Prasad had lost their jobs.

Now new loaders had taken their place. They hired a new batch of Baniharees. The CVO Colonel Sharma had been posted out so there was breath of freedom. It was rumored that the MD did not like the measures taken by the Colonel. In the beginning, the MD did try to put a leash on the rampant corruption, but this affected the Directors. First the CVO was ousted; then the MD retired. No one had yet gauged the new MD's policy. But he didn't seem to be particularly interested in rooting out corruption so everything was running as before.

Trivedi Sahib had not been keeping good health in recent times. His wife had gone to Bangalore to their son's place to take care of her daughter-in-law who was going to deliver a baby. But Mrs. Trivedi suddenly took ill and died. As Deepak Chatterjee was not very intimate with Trivedi, he refrained from asking any more details.

Deepak had come all the way from Maraal to Ramgadh so decided to see Mr. Trivedi at the hospital. RCL had a huge hospital located at Sunisarai, along the road to Dhanbad. When Deepak reached the hospital, he was told that Mr. Trivedi was in the ICU. He waited outside the ICU. He came across an old colleague, Manas Sengupta. Deepak asked Manas in which mine he was working in and was informed that he had retired. But while in service, he had got along very well with Trivedi and in deference to that he was at the hospital to render Mr. Trivedi his services.

Deepak inquired whether Trivedi's children were coming.

Manas told him that he had sent two telegrams and perhaps they were on their way to the hospital. They chatted about RCL. Deepak told him about Uttam Singh, the new GM and other matters. Manas warned him to be careful about Uttam Singh, who was known to be a very greedy man.

Deepak asked him about Trivedi's illness. Manas gave a perfunctory reply; says he has some blood related disease. The blood transfusion was under way in the ICU. Deepak did not ask for any more details.

When Deepak questioned Manas about the hospital expenses, Manas told him that it is a company-run hospital, hence subsidized. Deepak handed over the cash meant for Trivedi to Manas.

"Isn't this amount meant for the new GM, Uttam Singh?" Manas queried.

"I'll deal with that later. Right now, this money is required here."

Deepak came out of the hospital. He wondered whether Manas would put the cash he had given to him to good use. But Deepak knew Manas for many years and believed him to be a decent man. Even after retirement, he was willing to serve his ex-boss. Manas and Trivedi must have had financial dealings with each other, but more important was the fact that there was an element of affection for each other.

On the way back to Maraal, Deepak had a prick of conscience. He wondered whether he has to bear the consequences of for all his dishonest earnings. Was Trivedi's admission in the ICU a manifestation of someone's curse on him? Money for permits, for transport came from well-to-do people who could afford to pay or were forced to pay but even if they were giving it under pressure; they were driven by their selfish interests. Otherwise why would they give? The main issue for corruption is 'Time and hassel'. Everyone wants to get his/her work done quickly. The truck owner is in a hurry to load his truck and go out of the siding. The coal permit seekers want to avoid frequent trips to the Headquarters. People are willing to pay bribes so that their work gets done speedily.

But what about the plight of impersonators (Baniharees) The money I got from people like Ramnaresh and Ayodhya Prasad at that time, was a morsel out of the mouths of the poor impersonators (Baniharees). It was sheer exploitation of the needy. I have been witness to the kind of cruel treatment meted out to Jaggu Manjhi and Kali Manjhi by their masters Ramnaresh and Ayodhya Prasad. These poor impersonators (Baniharees) would never be able get free of their bonded labour. These powerful, influential masters harassed the wretched impersonators (Baniharees) through their *lathaiths* (Musclemen). These poor impersonators (Baniharees) must be cursing their masters.

I am sure these curses must be affecting all of us through people like Ayodhya Prasad and Ramnaresh, even the GM, Trivedi, must be getting affected. Otherwise, why would he be on his death bed so early in his life? Why did his wife die all of a sudden, for unknown reasons?

Then Deepak started thinking about his own life. He had no children. He and his wife had consulted so many specialists right up to Kolkata. They were told there was nothing wrong with both of them. Still, they could not bear a child. His wife was not in favour of adopting a child. She had hopes that one day she would bear a child, albeit late in life. Now she had almost reached her menopause. It occurred to Deepak that this might be the effect of the curses invoked upon him by the poor. Deepak was a devotee of Goddess Durga Devi, but so far he has not received her benediction.

Kirti was on one of her Sunday visits to Ramgadh. She had travelled in a Trax (jeep), which in the afternoon was not overloaded with passengers.

She thought of visiting Renuka. Being a Sunday, she would most likely be at home. But Kirti changed her mind as she did not want to spoil Renuka's family Sunday with her husband and daughter. Actually, Kirti longed to meet Aradhya, Renuka's daughter. She suppressed her desire and decided that when she would come again on official duty she could use the office transport to pay a visit.

Kirti wandered around Ramgadh all alone. She did not get the type of clothes she wanted, so she did not purchase anything. She thought she could do her shopping in Ranchi the following Sunday. Then to pass her time, she decided to watch a film. 'Veer Zara' that was running in the theatres then. The romantic scenes between Preiti Zinta and Shahrukh Khan reminded her of Piyush. She was wistful and when the song, '*humne kitne dard sahe tere liye' (how much grief I had to bear for you) played on screen,* she could not hold back her tears. The lady sitting next to her whispered to her husband in Bengali that the lady crying next to her perhaps had the same experience in her love affair (Aamhi bhabachi, ether kabhay kichu hoi chilo). Kirti overheard her and she controlled her tears.

When she came out of the cinema hall, after the end of movie, it began to rain. It wasn't a heavy shower, but there was a strong wind blowing. It was so strong that one had to hold on tight to the umbrella lest it might be carried away by the wind. She had somehow managed to hold her umbrella tight and reached the bus stand. The bus was full and people were riding on the top of the bus, somehow holding the ambrellas. She came out to the right side of bus-stand and saw that the jeeps were also over loaded. Then she went round to the left of the bus stand. There were auto and cycle rickshaws, but no one was willing to take her to Maraal. One of them agreed but asked for an exorbitant two hundred and fifty rupees. Kirti stood there, undecided. She felt like having a cup of tea so she walked into a restaurant close by. She had a plate of snacks (samosa) and then a cup of tea. She felt energized.

She saw an auto rickshaw pull up near the hotel. The passengers alighted and paid the driver. The driver was about to drive away in a hurry when she noticed that the driver had a familiar face. It was Baldev. She called him. He had to stop. He stepped out of the vehicle and greeted Kirti. Kirti felt a surge of anger and sadness within her but she kept a calm expression. She returned his greeting and asked whether he would drive her to Maraal.

Baldev replied that he could not because he had to take his daughter Munni to a birthday party and he was in a hurry to reach home. Kirti thought it was just an excuse to avoid the task. She asked him to look for any other auto driver who would drive her to Maraal.

Baldev negotiated with two or three other auto drivers but they refused to reduce the fare.

He walked back towards his auto when he found Kirti already sitting in it. He told her curtly that he really cannot go to Maraal as his family was expecting him home.

She told him it was alright; as it was raining, she would wait in the auto until she was able to get another auto. He made no reply and sat in the driver's seat. Both were calm and quiet.

She broke the silence, "Don't you ever feel like coming to Maraal?" Actually she wanted to ask him whether he no more felt attracted towards her.

He did not reply.

She asked him, "Since when have you started fearing your wife so much?"

"No madam, it's nothing like that." He replied.

She put her hand on his. "You can visit me sometimes, maybe during lunch time."

He said, "That's not possible. It is my business hour. Schools and colleges close at that time."

She felt hopeless, became quiet.

He said, "Madam, you must try to forget me."

Kirti replied, "I do try to forget you, but this flesh doesn't. I feel so lonely at night in the huge bungalow, I feel scared."

He said nothing.

She continued, "I know you want to sever our relationship. But at least for old times' sake, you can meet me once in a while and satisfy me."

Holding his hand tight she said, "I am sure you still have the sexual desire and the stamina. You need more than one woman to satisfy your lust. I too need you, want you."

Just then another auto came by. The driver was known to Baldev. Baldev convinced him to drive to Maraal. He agreed for a fare of Rs.100-

Baldev came back to his auto and found Kirti looking forlorn. Baldev told her that he had convinced another auto driver. She was reluctant to alight from his auto.

Baldev told Kirti," Madam, I want to say something—Please keep another companion in your quarters."

She retorted," Where can an old woman like me get another trustworthy man like you?"

Again he made no reply. She reluctantly stepped out of his auto and got into the waiting auto. Baldev approached the auto and thanked the driver.

Kirti kept looking at him and he avoided meeting her eye. The auto driver started the ignition and Baldev gestured him to drive away.

Baldev was staring at the departing auto in the distance. He was feeling a little guilty but he was now inured to this feeling. He had shifted to Ramgadh a year ago. Without Kirti's knowledge, his wife had secretly made up the mind to shift and implemented the plan with all temperory provisions.

He had bought a plot of land on Rajrappa road. People had slowly begun to settle in that area. One of his wife's acquaintances had come to reside there. Water and electricity connections were also being given.

Four years ago he had quit riding the cycle rickshaw and had bought an auto rickshaw. Kirti Madam had helped him to obtain a bank loan. With an increased income, he had paid off the cost of the plot and had started saving up for the construction of three rooms. At first he had only laid the foundation for which he sometimes would dig the earth himself. He had told Kirti that once the house was ready, he would rent it out. Kirti was unaware of the real intention of Baldev's wife and by the time it dawned on her, it was too late.

It was the wily Munni, Baldev's eldest daughter, who was the instigator against Kirti. She was finding it too confining to live in Kirti's quarters. Until she was ten years old, she would hang around Kirti, calling her '*Mausi, Mausi*' (Maternal aunt). Kirti aunt would also get her a lot of nice clothes, bangles, necklaces, ear rings. Naturally, Munni used to be very happy with Kirti.

When she reached the fifth standard and joined another school, there was a change in her attitude. She began to understand things, especially when her friends asked her about her aunt (Mausi). They had put strange ideas in her head. Munni had begun to understand another kind of man-woman relationship. She began to look at her aunt and her father from that new perspective. She started asking her mother uncomfortable questions. The mother would shut her up angrily. But Munni kept asking subtle questions.

Kirti never realized at first that Munni was slowly drifting apart from her. Although she continued showering Munni with gifts of clothes and trinkets, she failed to observe Munni's diminishing enthusiasm in all those things. She thought that Munni enjoyed the company of her friends more than her aunt's.

It took a long time for Kirti to realize that the construction of the house in Ramgadh was a precursor to other plans. She had obliged Baldev and his family with so much financial help that it never occurred to her that they might someday cheat her and desert her.

Munni and her mother wanted a separation from Kirti. But they did not say it aloud. Days passed on. The house construction was complete. Madam had introduced them to banking earlier so they knew about Recurring/Fixed Deposits. All this money came in handy for construction of house. Baldev's wife had apprised Baldev about the fact that Munni's friends were teasing her about her aunt or *Mausi*.

Baldev did not pay any attention in the beginning. When his wife proposed that instead of giving their new house on rent, they should shift there themselves, Baldev was stunned, amazed, that such an illiterate woman could come up with such a brilliant idea.

The problem was how to convey it to Kirti. Baldev lacked the temerity to do it. Then Munni insisted that she wanted to study in Ramgadh. She had a friend studying in Ramgadh. Munni was now in Class VIII and quite mature. Munni's mother used this as an excuse to talk to Kirti about shifting to Ramgadh. Kirti lost her temper and abused Baldev's wife. Kirti's ego was terribly hurt. She felt insulted that she was being cheated by this family whom she had literally picked up from the pits and provided them with money, and with a comfortable home. She called Baldev's wife ungrateful and selfish.

Baldev's wife also retaliated with unpleasant words. Baldev was not in the house at that time. She told Kirti that she had seen with her own eyes how her husband would sneak into Kirti's room. What agony she experienced then? She was also human after all. So what if she belonged to low strata, she also had sentiments. And what would happen to Munni's future? She would have to get married at an early age as per tribal customs. It would be difficult and awkward to explain Kirti's place in their family

A month passed in this unpleasant atmosphere. Kirti tried her best to persuade Baldev not to shift to Ramgadh, but all in vain. Baldev's wife was adamant. She just loaded the auto rickshaw with the household things and headed straight for Ramgadh. The auto made three round trips transporting the clothes, buckets, mattresses, and some utensils that she had bought herself. She had already made temperory provisions by purchasing them and hidden from Kirti. She did not take the bed, table or those things that had been provided by Kirti. They were made to do with a wick (kerosene) stove at first and then bought a gas stove.

Baldev's wife was very happy to set up her new home. Munni was extremely delighted. Only Baldev was rather sad. He fell at Kirti's feet when they finally left her home, in last trip of auto. No one was watching, so Kirti held Baldev in her arms and both of them wept bitterly.

Although their relationship was solely a physical one, over the years, they did feel a certain emotional attachment towards each other. Kirti realized that Baldev was helpless, but her own loneliness bothered her. For a second time in her life, she had been cheated in a relationship, but there was nothing she could do.

All these memories haunted Kirti as the auto rickshaw sped towards Maraal. It was still raining, but it was a gentle rain. The auto reached Maraal and the driver asked which direction she wanted to go. His question jolted her out of her reverie. She gave him the address and direction. On reaching her quarters, she paid the auto driver and walked towards the door, not bothering to open her umbrella. She opened the gate. It was dark near the door. She opened the lock on her door by the light of the street lamp. She switched on the light inside, closed the door, threw herself on the sofa and wept inconsolably. She stuffed her pallav into her mouth to muffle her sobs. She did not want her neighbours to hear her crying.

She missed Piyush terribly that day. She had flung herself into a life of sensual pleasure only to be able to forget Piyush, like some sort of escape mechanism. She had deliberately got into physical relationships, just to prove to herself that she could live life on her own terms, without a crutch, a husband or ties of love. Piyush has made such a hollowness in her life, that she went for passionate adventures, not bothering for society in general.

But she realized that unless a relationship is accepted by society, it cannot last. Only when there is social sanction to a relationship, there might be less loneliness and more family support. And if one has children, then the past is more easily forgotten. She had been totally disillusioned in her belief that one can live a wanton life on one's own terms.

She felt that, sex therapy can not be a solution for broken heart. The men in gereral go for alcohol on such desperate situations. She could not opt for it, because she had not even tested it. The need of the body was compromised with the morality of society. The young and energetic years are gone where sex was an escape and enjoyment. Now the shadowing years are ahead desiring companionship, love and understanding.

Piyush had cheated her, but he had been her first and her only love." Why does a person fall in love at all?" She asked herself often. "Where did this intense, all consuming love spring from?" But at the end, what is left is only the memory of love, the heartache, the empty eyes and the endless waiting to see the loved one at least one more time!. At this juncture of life, it seems that companionship is needed, but for her, there was a total misfortune.

Piyush had practically gone out of her life forever. There was no way she could ever see him or meet him again. Such a meeting would have been futile too. She felt that she has failed in her life in both aspects, that are love and sex.

It was as if in the waning years of her life, the wounds in her heart had festered again and overwhelmed her with the gushing flow of grief. She feared she would go mad with her mental agony. She decided it was time to take control of her feelings and behave sensibly.

She got up and went into the kitchen. There was a small prayer room there. She stood in front of the image of Kali Mata (goddess) and joined her hands in suppliance. Tears rolled down her cheeks. She lit an oil lamp and stared into the flame. She felt like a sad oil lamp herself, burning until the fuel lasted and then get snuffed out one day.

Ramlal sat at home. Parbati and Manoj were out at work. Ramlal was suffering from *asthma*. He would get frequent bouts of cough. He could get medical treatment at the Coalmine hospital on the basis of Parbati's Dependent Card. It was three years since he had retired. Janaki had got him to quit smoking *beedis* a long time ago.

When Manoj had got his Diploma, Ramlal made a lot of efforts to get Manoj the job of a foreman. He had even made the rounds of Ichotu Area Office. He was willing to spend money if required. He had judiciously invested his Provident Fund and Gratuity in Fixed Deposits for varying periods. He would get quarterly interests on some of these.

Some amounts had been fixed for three year terms. Although he was illiterate, he had learnt about banking from an old colleague who had been a supervisor.

Ramlal was worried about Manoj's future. So he was willing to spend his retirement funds. All the vacancies for 'foreman' at the various mines in Maraal, Gola and Chutkakhana in Ichotu Area had been filled up. There was no more hiring for the foreman's post. But there were some new ones for the post of 'Trainee Electrician'. Actually, Manoj wished to go to Ranchi or to Tatanagar and work as an engineer; but his family was against it, especially his grandmother Janaki, who doted on him.

With a heavy heart Manoj had to give in to family pressure and change his mind about going to Ranchi. Ramlal did not have to spend anything. Everyone was happy that Manoj was going to be with the family in Maraal.

Ramlal had to vacate his quarters on retirement. One of Ramlal's acquaintances, an Operator, had shifted into those quarters with his family. A partition wall was erected between Parvathi's quarter and Ramlal's old quarters. Ramlal was trying hard to get the quarters allotted for Manoj.

Jaggu Manjhi would visit Ramlal often. His visits became more frequent after Radha had passed away. Usually, he would ask Ramlal to come out and they would both have tea at the wayside tea stall. But sometimes Ramlal would offer tea in the house. If jaggu was coming straight from work, his clothes would be dirty and he would decline to go into the house. But on holidays, he would be dressed in decent clothes. Parvati would invite him in and offer tea and snacks. Everyone sympathized with him for having lost Radha. No one objected to his visits at first but later Janaki had suspicions that Parbati was paying undue attention to Jaggu. She felt that Parbati might be attracted to Jaggu. Jaggu however, had no such intention. Janaki felt that Parbati might be feeling deprived of conjugal pleasure because of her husband Shivlal's early death. Although she was in her forties, she looked young and energetic. Perhaps she still yearned for sexual fulfillment. Janaki would therefore prefer to send Ramlal out with Jaggu.

The Operator, who lived next door was promoted and now entitled to a bigger, 'A' type quarters. Since he was vacating the miner's quarter, Ramlal tried to get that allotted for Manoj. Manoj had also become a permanent employee and was entitled to accommodation. In this context, Ramlal met Kirti. Kirti and her staff had a soft corner for diseased Shivlal's family because he had worked as an officer earlier. Ramlal took advantage of this softness and tried to make it work for Manoj. He succeeded and Manoj was allotted the accommodation next door. Again the wall was dismantled and a door fitted between Parbati's and Manoj's quarters. Actually this was the third time that such a renovation was made. When Lakshmi and Saraswati used to come for spending time at their parents' home, the house would seem too small. The door would then be opened. On Raksha Bandhan and Bhaiyya Dooj or Chhath, Manoj would bring his sisters home. Parbati would be very happy to have her daughters at home and she would miss her husband at such times.

Now with Manoj settled in life, the family wanted him to get married. Manoj was not ready to tie the knot so early in life. But his grandmother Janaki explained that as a boy, he was already eligible for marriage as per tribal customs. When one foreman, an old acquaintance of Ramlal came with a proposal for his daughter, Parbati's happiness knew no bounds. Besides, the girl was known to them. The family had earlier lived in Maraal before the foreman's transfer to Gola as an Engineer.

There was a simple marriage ceremony. The coming of the grand daughter-in-law eased Janaki's household work. Parbati was a working woman, so Janaki had to handle all the chores. Now she had a helping hand in the form of her grand daughter-in-law.

The new daughter-in-law got accustomed to the family. But she resented one thing and that was the Sunday alcohol drinking routine. Although they drank in moderation, along with the meat, she did not like it. Her father had stopped this tribal custom in her parents' home. Her grandmother had been the one responsible for putting a stop to the custom despite her grandfather's strong objection. Here, she feared that Manoj's grandfather, Ramlal might also want to continue with the custom. Some months into the marriage, she casually mentioned to Parbati that back in her home, this ritual of drinking liquor together as a family had been done away with. Parbati understood that the daughter-in-law did not like their drinking.

Parbati also thought about it for a while. Then one Sunday, the family sat down to lunch as usual. Rice and tomato chutney had been served on a plate. Mutton curry was served in a bowl. Janaki, Parbati's mother-in-law asked why the liquor had not been bought. Parbati said it had not been bought and neither would it be bought again. No one in the house would henceforth consume liquor. That was her firm decision. Every one stared at her, stunned. But she stood firm like a rock.

After lunch, Ramlal sat there scowling and angry. Manoj tried to appease him." Grandpa, your health is deteriorating these days."

"A couple of gulps of liquor are not going to kill me," Ramlal retorted.

Manoj kept quiet for a few moments. Then he said, "Don't you know how father died. Had he restricted himself to drinking only on Sundays, he would have been alive. But this liquor thing is very bad."

"This is all nonsense."

Manoj said, "Do you wish that I too start drinking outside the house regularly? My friends have offered me whisky so many times. But I remember father, and control myself. Do you want me to be like my father (Baba)?" He began to cry. Ramlal too became emotional and hugged and consoled his grandson.

Manoj clung on to his grandfather. Parbati and Janaki watched the scene from a distance.

Ramlal conceded that what Parbati had done was right. She should have taken that step earlier. The mind cannot rid itself of habits. But sometime or the other, one has to get rid of a bad habit.

Every one heaved a sigh of relief. Manoj's wife was delighted.

One day Kirti got a phone call from Renuka. "You haven't called me of late, Kirti."

"Yes, I was a bit busy."

"Didn't you make a trip to Ramgadh?" Renuka asked.

"I did come once on a Sunday, but since Collector Sahib would also have been at home, I decided not to disturb you." Kirti replied.

"Well, your niece remembers you often. She remembers the chocolates you give her." Renuka told.

"Oh, that's nice that she remembers her aunt. I too miss her. Tell her that I will meet her soon and get her chocolates too." Kirti's eyes filled with tears as she said this. Her voice became slightly hoarse.

Renuka asked with concern, "Are you alright?"

"Oh yes, I am fine," Kirti said taking control of herself.

Renuka said, "Come over to my place this Saturday afternoon. Kripal Singh has to attend a meeting in Hazaribaug. I have not been invited. It is departmental meeting. He will be going alone."

"Oh sure, I will definitely come."

Renuka hung up the phone.

Kirti reached Renuka's house on Saturday afternoon, after attending usual half day work. Aradhya came scampering to her and Kirti picked her up in her arms. Kirti took out two Cadbury chocolate bars from her purse and gave them to Aradhya. Aradhya gave her a kiss and said, "Thank you."

Renuka instructed Aradhya, "You can have only one chocolate today. Eat the other one tomorrow or it will rot your teeth, you know that, don't you?"

Aradhya nodded her head.

Renuka and Kirti went into the drawing room. Renuka switched on the Cartoon channel for Aradhya and kept it on 'Mute' mode.

Just then Buaji entered the room. Kirti got up and touched her feet. Buaji said, "It's alright, you don't have to do that."

They began to chat. Renuka told Kirti that Aradhya had grown very naughty recently. She liked her Papa more because he pampered her a lot.

Kirti enquired about Renuka's work schedule.

Renuka said it was all fine." I was awarded a medal on 15th August and my staff is very happy about it. I had arranged a tea party for them as a celebration. I told them that I owed the medal to them. If they had not supported her and helped her to maintain law and order, she would not have received the medal."

Kirti cautioned her, "Despite the medal, I suggest you keep a watchful eye on the law and order situation in the district. I mean, at least in my Coalfield. You see, once again there is a rise in thefts and corruption. Some days back there was a very strict CVO, who had tried to put an end to it all..."

"Look, when I catch them red-handed on the road, I will take action. I will also act upon the tips I get from my informers, but I cannot go into the minds of people and change their corrupt and thieving attitude. There are limitations on our operations. If there is a systematic corruption, I find it difficult to track it and stop it "Renuka explained.

"That is true. The Colonel Sahib, who was the CVO, also said the same thing at the meeting. For a brief period, people had become afraid of disciplinary and official action against corruption. But after the Colonel left, this evil of corruption has raised its head like a cobra." Said Kirti.

"Oh, so we are back to the problem. Even the impersonation (Baniharee) system...?" Renuka asked.

"Yes, Did I not tell you how the Colonel had picked up each impersonators (Baniharee) and straightaway had the Baniharee's master, the government employee, dismissed from the job? Perhaps you remember the case of Jaggu Manhji..." Kirti told.

"Yes, I do remember. Radha's husband. Just a moment, the phone is ringing, I have to answer the phone. I will take it in my room. It must be from Headquarters." Renuka told.

She hurried into the bedroom; she didn't even hear Kirti saying, "Alright."

Kirti started remembering the details of Jaggu's case.

Colonel Sharma and Major Swami had become a famous pair in those days. People at the RCL Coalfields would jokingly call them '*Do Jasoos*' (Two detectives). Ever since the MD had given them a free hand, corruption cases had abated at the Coal Security Check Points. There was also a change in the 'Same Three Quotation Procedure' for Purchase and Repair jobs. The tenders for quotations would be advertised on the notice board at least fifteen days in advance. E-tendering was introduced in the Civil Department. Contractors and Suppliers had started browsing the websites. Some unemployed youth in Jharkhand had started co-operative institutions. The State government had proposed and recommended that these co-operatives should be given work contracts. These youth with the help of computers, and with the help of E-tendering, got work contracts in the Civil Departments. They got the support from the local MLA's. The State Government was also paying special attention to eradicate corruption and Jharkhand being a newly created state the authorities were trying to provide employment to the youth of Jharkhand. To fulfil their objective, officers from state government were in constant negotiations with the Coalfields authorities. Because of that established contractors and Coal Mafia felt a little threatened and their activities and business got restricted.

The workers employing the impersonators (Baniharees) were facing a lot of problems under the strict vigil of the Colonel and the Major duo and those working as railway wagon loaders, at almost all the mines were removed from their jobs. Some clerks working at the weigh bridges were transferred out of some mines and loading supervisors like Ashok Kumar were demoted and transferred to non-sensitive posts.

Existing contractors for transport of coal were replaced. Some ingenious contractors opened new companies not in Ichotu area but in different places like Gumla, or Latehaar and they just exchanged their work areas. Some big contractors did have the tacit blessings of higher officials of the Coalfields.

The Naxalites (terrorists) held sway over some parts of Jharkhand. All the government Officers and Contractors had to pay the Naxalites a monthly fee. It used to be collected under the garb of a religious or social cause. If this extortion money was not paid, then the rebel contractor or concerned officer would be kidnapped and the family would have to pay an enormous ransom for their release. If some family approached the police for help, then the kidnapped victim's corpse would be found on the main road, thus most often the people found it safer to pay the monthly extortion fee.

Some new, young contractors replaced the old established ones. One of these new contractors had to suffer a tragic fate. He failed to pay the Naxalites the amount they demanded so he was kidnapped. Some other young men complained this to the police and the young contractor was murdered by the Naxalites. At such times, the old contractors once again took their places. This incident took place in Latehaar. Renuka read about it in the newspaper and felt very sad. Renuka was successful in not allowing the Naxalites to get a foothold in Ramgadh and won a lot of praise in the Ministry at Ranchi.

The General Managers of the area in which the Colonel and Major duo conducted a series of raids were also shaken up. They approached the Directors for help. The flow of money to them got considerably reduced resulting in Directors getting smaller amounts. The consequence of all this was that Colonel Sharma was transferred after tenure of three years and a more pliable CVO was brought in. Major Swami was also transferred to a new company. It was in one of these raids that Ramnaresh and his associates lost their jobs. Kirti advised Ramnaresh to work himself at the mine for a few days and keep Jaggu away. Ramnaresh did not have the physical strength to put in hard labour of lifting coal baskets and was too complacent with the feeling that he could wield a lot of financial power to get out of any situation.

But one day all of a sudden, a big team from the Vigilance Department arrived at the Railway Siding. The team consisted of officers from various departments like Personnel, Security, Finance and most importantly, the Vigilance department. Area Security Officer, Neeraj Kumar was called to join in later. Manager Prabhunath Singh, Sales manager Deepak Chatterjee and Project Officer Santosh Kumar Sinha were petrified. The necessary papers were drawn for suspending immediately Loading Supervisor Ashok Kumar Jha. In the midst of all this turmoil, suspension orders for Ramnaresh, Janu Prasad and Ayodhya Prasad and others were also put out. They were charge-sheeted and the inquiry into their case was wrapped up within three months. Ramnaresh tried to seek Madan Oza's help. But the CVO was having the Managing Director's support and none dared to quash the case or bribe any officer to dilute the case.

The case papers pertaining to earlier case involving Ramnaresh were also amalgamated with this new charge. Impersonators (Baniharees) like Jaggu Manjhi, Kali Manjhi and Narsa Munda and other had also been trapped and their statements attested by the thumb impressions of all three. Madan Oza's influence didn't work this time. Madan could not approach Satish Trivedi, General Manager (sales) who himself was reeling under an inquiry instituted against him. Some of the scandals in his department had been reported in the newspapers.

Some people tried to use political influence but that too was of no use. A new rule came into force with the consent of the RCL Board regarding transfers from 'lucrative posts' or sensitive posts, according to which all those officers and clerks and secretariat staff holding a post for more than fifteen years would be immediately removed from these post and transferred. The departments that were most vulnerable to corruption like Personnel, Sales, Purchase and Finance were especially targeted.

Madan Oza tried to use political influence in Ramnaresh's case, but it did not prove to be much helpful. It only prolonged the case. There was a delay in the termination order. Ramnaresh filed his case in the Labour Court. He pleaded with the RCL that he should be allowed to retain his government accommodation until the pendency of the labour court case and was given a six-month extension to live in those quarters. These six months proved very tragic for Radha. There was Holi festival during this period.

When Jaggu got caught in the vigilance raid, he was very badly beaten up with sticks by Ramnaresh's goons, Naval Prasad and Suresh Singh. He was laid down for a week as a result of the bruises he suffered. Radha invoked a spate of curses on Ramnaresh. One of her foxy neighbours conveyed this to Ramnaresh's wife.

After a week, when Jaggu's bruises were somewhat healed went to the coal loading point. A new contractor named Joginder Singh had taken charge of the transport contract. He was in need of workers and so Jaggu got the job as a daily wage labour. Jaggu was a hard worker and Joginder Singh was very happy with him.

Ramnaresh would also come to the loading point. He would oversee the loading process at Madan Oza's loading point. Sometimes he and Jaggu would come face to face. Jaggu would greet him politely but Ramnaresh would rudely brush it off. Naval Prasad and Suresh Singh would also join Ramnaresh at the loading point after finishing of supplying milk to the households. Ramnaresh would go home after the arrival of his goons.

Several days passed uneventfully. One day Jaggu felt like going home so he made a trip to Kundapara. His brothers gave him a cold welcome. They did not give immediately charge of their room. Jaggu's brother's wife was stingy in serving them food and so Radha tried to set up her own stove and cook a meal. Jaggu inquired from the Patwari about his share of the field and paid a visit to the plot. He believed that his brothers might have tilled his land but learned that some moneylender was tilling his land. He was told that his brothers had mortgaged Jaggu's plot and had accumulated so much interest on it and there was no way they could redeem it from the moneylender. When Jaggu confronted his brothers about this, they said their mother had put her thumb impression on the mortgage so he should ask his deceased mother for an explanation.

The eldest brother told Jaggu that they owed the money lender rupees thirty five thousand. Jaggu should pay the amount and have his land released. Jaggu raised a hue and cry but it had no effect on the brothers. Radha also spoke in strong words.

Sonu admonished her that women should not interfere in men's affairs. They also got into an argument over it.

Jaggu returned to Maraal within three days, a broken, helpless man. He gave up all hopes of ever going to Kundapara. He had lost his mother; his brothers had cheated him out of his property. Radha was not allowed to pamper or endear Keshu's children. They also stopped calling her aunt 'Kaki Ma'. They were sent to the neighbours to play and warned to keep away at a distance from Radha. Radha felt deeply hurt.

Jaggu went back to his humble existence. He would live frugally, save money and pay off the interest. Radha was a pillar of strength to him. They stopped buying new clothes. Some women in whose houses she worked would give Radha their old, discarded sarees. Sometimes Radha would unabashedly ask for old clothes for Jaggu. Sometimes these would hang loose on Jaggu's body. He never liked them so would get them altered from a tailor.

That accursed Holi (festival of colors) occurred in those months. Jaggu's worker-friends had taken him to the loading point and played Holi with just water. Someone had brought opium tablets and some others had brought liquor. Despite Jaggu's protests, he had been forced to drink liquor and swallow an opium tablet. They were all slightly inebriated and went around a few places splashing people with colours they had got from the people only.

Before leaving the house in the morning, Jaggu smeared some sindoor (vermilion) on Radha's cheek. Since there was no colour powder in the house, Radha blackened her hands with coal and smeared it on Jaggu's cheek and laughed playfully. That was her last laugh!

Radha had to leave the house early to cope with her work. She cooked rice and potato curry before leaving the house. As it was Holi, she got some sweet or savoury to eat in every house she worked. She thought of Jaggu every time she was given something.

Ramnaresh's two brothers-in-law (Wife's brothers) had come to celebrate Holi festival at their sister's house. One of them was married but had left his wife at home to be with his parents. They had been given an affectionate welcome by Ramnaresh's wife. She got up early and made snacks (Kachories) for them. Sweetmeats had already been purchased the previous day. She had prepared *Thandai opium drink by* mixing Bhang (ground poppy seeds/ opium) with milk and a lot of dry fruits like almonds, raisins and cashew nuts. Her two brothers had been relishing glass after glass of this drink. Ramnaresh's henchmen, Naval Prasad and Suresh Singh were not to be seen. Naval Prasad had gone to his hometown and Suresh Singh was on a fun ride with his friends around the town.

Ramnaresh pulled out a bottle of whisky from the cupboard. The brothers-in-law were excited about the English liquor. Combined with the Bhang (opium), the cocktail liquor became a heady brew and they got intoxicated.

Outside the house, Ramnaresh's wife Kamini was playing Holi with some women. She saw Radha from a distance. An evil idea struck her. She called out Radha. The other women had started leaving by then. She invited Radha into the house on the pretext of giving her some sweets. Radha declined, but Kamini took her in forcibly by holding her hand. Radha tried to free her hand. Some neighbours were watching it with fun and as it was Holi, no one objected.

As they entered the courtyard, all male eyes were centered on Radha. Ramnaresh's wife first smeared red colour on Radha who reciprocated the gesture. Then Kamini gave her a packet of Kachori and sweets. As Radha prepared to leave, Kamini told her to sit there and eat it. Kamini told her that she would give her another packet for Jaggu.

By then Kamini's brothers and Ramnaresh were totally inebriated. The older brother-in-law got up and said to his sister, "Sister, I too want to apply colour on this lissome lass."

Radha quickly retorted, "I am not a lass."

Radha tried to run away, but Kamini's brother held her from the back. Ramnaresh's wife did not stop her brother. She brought forth the plate of colours. The brother took a handful of colors and put it on Radha's cheek and he tried to put it into her blouse.

The younger brother got excited too and rushed forward to close the main gate. Radha tried to escape from the grip of elder brother and began to shout for help. Kamini told her that it was alright for her to play a little Holi. By then the other brother had also gripped Radha. She desperately tried to resist but proved too weak in front of their brute strength. She started crying out aloud but then elder brother-in-law put his hand on her mouth. Both brothers picked her up and took her inside. Ramnaresh's wife made a weak objection trying to stop them. Ramnaresh, in his drunken state, muttered, "Jaggu, Holi Mubarak, (greeting for Holi festival)" and clapped his hands.

The brothers bolted the bedroom door and closed the windows. They tore off Radha's clothes. They first slapped her repeatedly and then threw her on the bed and tied her mouth with a cloth. They pinned her down and raped her. Radha struggled against them but became a helpless victim, crying and pleading.

Outside Ramnaresh's wife was sipping some Thandai. Ramnaresh sat beside her, patting her shoulder as if to compliment her. He forcibly put a glass of whisky to her lips and made her have a sip although she refused.

After a while, the elder brother-in-law came out and gestured for Ramnaresh to go in. At first, Ramnaresh was hesitant. He was afraid to go in the presence of his wife, Kamini. So the brother-in-law cleverly took his sister into the kitchen on the pretext of wanting one more snack (kachori). Kamini was also a bit drunk by then. The younger brother-in-law came out of the bed room after finishing his fiendish act. He held Ramnaresh's hand and led him into the bedroom. Radha was trying to cover her nakedness with a bed sheet that she pulled out from under the pillow. Just as she was about to wrap herself, Ramnaresh entered. Radha became livid on seeing him. The brother-in-law pushed Ramnaresh inside and bolted the door from outside. Radha spit at Ramnaresh's face. Ramnaresh hit her on her face. He kicked her. Radha groaned with pain. She had lost all her strength.

In his drunken state, Ramnaresh forced himself on her. While raping her, in a drunken state he was uttering abuses to Radha and Jaggu. He finished his act quickly. He banged the door. His wife opened the door. Radha had wrapped a sheet around her and was weeping. Ramnaresh's wife threw a saree and a blouse at her and left the room. Radha put on the clothes and limped towards the door. Ramnaresh's wife opened the main gate for her. She gave Radha three 500-rupee notes (1500 rupees) and told her to keep quiet or else her husband would cut Jaggu into pieces. Radha walked out of the gate, spat at Ramnaresh's wife and threw the 500-rupee notes at her. She tried to run from there but her feet did not have the strength left in them. The neighbours watched in consternation.

Radha struggled to reach her hut. Jaggu had not yet returned home. She drew the curtain close. She drank a glass of water and wept bitterly. She spotted the kerosene bottle in the corner. She got up and picked up the match box kept near the image of Kali Mata. She joined her hands in obeisance to the goddess and then sprinkled kerosene all over her body muttering, "Mother Goddess, Mother Goddess" and struck a match to burn herself as she felt her defiled body was no more fit for Jaggu. The hut also caught fire. She suppressed her cry of pain at first. But then she screamed in agony. The neighbours came running and doused the fire with water. But Radha had suffered severe burns already. Someone went out to look for Jaggu and they brought him home. Radha barely managed to tell him that the bastard Ramnaresh had raped her. Jaggu picked up his axe and wanted to go and kill Ramnaresh, but Ramlal persuaded him to take Radha to a hospital first. Parbati also arrived and wrapped Radha in another saree. They picked up Radha and took her to the hospital. Ramlal however headed towards Kirti's bungalow. He narrated the incident to Kirti. Kirti knew it was a police case and immediately telephoned Renuka and requested her to direct the police station to take action. She handed over a slip to Ramlal to facilitate Radha's admission in the hospital.

The Compounder at the RCL hospital was unwilling to admit Radha. He said that neither Radha nor Jaggu were on the Coalfield employee roll and so were not authorized this facility. He asked them to take her to a private hospital or a government -run hospital. Everyone looked for the doctor but he too was busy celebrating Holi. But the lady doctor was at home. Ramlal showed her Kirti's chit. The lady doctor quickly called for a nurse and began treatment. The lady doctor was a decent lady. She washed Radha's burns and applied an antiseptic cream. Radha was given a gown to wear. Parbati was helping out with that. The doctor knew it would be a police case so she went on making official notes of the bruises and marks on Radha's body. She made a medical report noting down the evidence of rape. She started administering a medicine through the saline. She was of the opinion as it was burn case, the patient should be admitted in the ICU at the District Hospital as soon as possible. Meanwhile, she prepared the relevant papers.

As a result of the call from Renuka, the Maraal police had to go over to the hospital and make preliminary enquiries. They reached late. By then the news about Radha had spread in Maraal

Colony. On learning that Radha had tried to immolate herself and was admitted in a hospital, Ramnaresh was jolted out of his drunken stupor. Then he was told that the police were also at the hospital. Terrified, Ramnaresh and his two brothers-in-law ran away on his motorcycle. Ramnaresh's wife quickly tidied up the room and swept it. She had hidden Radha's torn saree under a dung heap. She put a fresh sheet on the bed.

Jaggu and Ramlal told the police that Ramnaresh had raped Radha, so Radha had immolated herself. The lady doctor was not permitting police to meet Radha. The police told Jaggu and Ramlal to come over to the police station and lodge an F. I. R. Ramlal took the initiative to do it. He found a willing supporter in Kali Manjhi. Jaggu and Parbati stayed by Radha's side.

Kirti visited the hospital and realized the gravity of the crime. She discussed with the doctor. They were trying to locate the ambulance driver. Arrangements were under way to transport Radha to the Government Hospital in Ramgadh. Kirti apprised Renuka of the situation over the telephone. She requested Renuka to make a call to the hospital so that Radha could get adequate and quick treatment.

The police reached Ramnaresh's house. His wife told them that he was away to Ramgadh since morning to play Holi. She said she did not know who Radha was. No lady by that name had come to her house. She said they could ask the neighbours for confirmation. She was confident that the neighbours feared Ramnaresh. Suresh Singh stood at the door with the batton menacingly so none of the neighbours dared to open his mouth to speak. The police reported the entire matter to Renuka SP over phone from the police station. There was no lady constable at the Maraal police station so the police had a problem arresting Kamini, Ramnaresh's wife. Renuka instructed them to continue looking for Ramnaresh. Radha was shifted to Ramgadh in an ambulance and admitted into an ICU. She was put on medicated saline I. V.

Renuka arrived at the hospital at 4 o'clock in the evening. The atmosphere became very tense on SP Sahiba's arrival. Kirti was already there. Both discussed the matter with the doctor. Renuka patiently listened to what Jaggu had to say. Radha corroborated as best as she could, all that Jaggu narrated to Renuka. She especially verified the fact that Ramnaresh's wife had invited her in to have Holi sweets and her brothers had forced themselves on Radha. Jaggu cried inconsolably as he narrated the incident. He pleaded that his wife be saved somehow; he could not live without her.

At six o'clock in the evening, Renuka arrived again at the hospital with the Magistrate. Kirti had told Radha to gather all the strength she could to record her statement. Then in the presence of two witnesses and the Magistrate, Radha made her statement. Her thumb impression was taken on the statement. Jaggu, Ramlal and Kirti were waiting outside. Renuka had taken prior permission to be present at the recording of the statement.

At night, Radha's condition became worse. Jaggu and Ramlal were at the hospital. Renuka took Kirti along to her own house. She asked Kirti to wait at the house while she made a trip to her office. Early in the morning, Renuka had driven to Maraal in her police van. Kirti was also with her. Kirti walked to her bungalow. Renuka went directly to the police station. The inspector was not in office. She sent for him. She checked the F. I. R and investigation report. The Inspector got scared on seeing the SP. He still seemed to be nursing his Holi hangover.

The police team arrived at Ramnaresh's house. Ramnaresh's wife got into an argument with them at the doorstep. Renuka had brought three lady constables with her. Strongman Suresh Singh was helpless when he saw such a big police posse. Kamini tried to prevent the police from entering the house, but the lady constables gave her two tight slaps. She began to cry. They asked her where her two brothers were. She said she didn't n know. She swore by the names of strange goddesses and declared that Radha never came to the house and that Ramnaresh and her brothers were at a friend's place in Ramgadh since the previous morning. She said she did not know the friend's name. She said they could ask the neighbours. The neighbours had ventured out of their houses by this time.

Renuka inspected the house. Although the room had been swept, she found some broken bangle pieces under the cupboard. The top sheet looked clean but when she pulled out the one underneath, she saw tell-tale signs of the incident. There were traces of semen on the sheet. She quickly put the sheet in a plastic bag and sealed the bag. She was unable to find Radha's clothes. In her statement, Radha had said that the saree she was wearing when she set herself on fire was the one given by Ramnaresh's wife. That saree was found in the hospital at Maraal. The blouse had been charred almost completely. A constable had found broken pieces of bangles in the garbage heap behind the house. Renuka came to the buffalo-shed. Her suspicions were aroused and she poked through the dung heaps with a stick. She found some pieces of cloth there, when the constables upturned the whole heap, they found the clothes. These were also taken into custody and kept in a plastic bag and sealed. Renuka then dangled the bag in front of Ramnaresh's wife and asked whether Radha had been there or not. She began to cry but did not answer the question.

Again she was asked about the whereabouts of Ramnaresh. She said that she did not know. Suresh Singh also got a few blows by stick, but he denied any knowledge of Ramnaresh's location. He said Ramnaresh is with some friends but does not know exactly where. Then Ramnaresh's wife was shown the arrest warrant. There was no way she could read and understand. Renuka had already issued arrest warrants against four of them. Ramnaresh's wife was told that she had to go to the Ramgadh Police Station. She fell at Renuka's feet, but she was bundled into the waiting van.

Renuka then directed her attention to the neighbours. She very calmly told them to cooperate with the police. One over smart neighbor said that he did not know anything. Renuka gave him one blow with her stick and bundled him into the van. Then she began to talk with the others. They started speaking freely. They said they had seen Ramnaresh's wife holding Radha's hand and taking her in. Two people had seen Radha limping home after the incident. Renuka told them to come to the police station and endorse their statements. She assured them that they would not come to any harm. They agreed. The man in the van was let out.

At the hospital, Radha was struggling with her life. She had suffered 75% burns but the doctors were trying to do their best to save her. Jaggu sat there, feeling distraught. Ramlal had with a lot of difficulty, managed to feed him some biscuits and tea. Parbati had brought some breakfast for Ramlal and Jaggu.

Radha's tears came gushing on seeing Parbati. Parbati consoled her. Radha held onto Parbati's hand for a long time. Parbati had sent Ramlal home to Maraal to freshen up. She would wait at the hospital till he returned. Ramlal had taken the addresses of Jaggu's brothers and of Radha's family and had sent them telegrams.

At the Maraal police station, Renuka recorded the statements of Ramnaresh's neighours. Ramnaresh's wife refused to tell where Ramnaresh was. Since Suresh Singh was not around when the incident took place, he was going to be let free. But they were still holding him at the police station in the hope that he might give Ramnaresh's address.

Renuka then went to Ramgadh. She sent Ramnaresh's wife and Suresh Singh to the police station. Ramnaresh's wife was put in the prison cell. Two lady constables were asked to beat her up a little. Then Suresh Singh was threatened of third degree if he did not give the required information. At first he was defiant but when he was threatened with custodial treatment, he blurted out that Ramnaresh had two or three very close friends in Ramgadh. Of these, Ramnaresh used to visit Madan Oza frequently. Ramnaresh handled Oza's coal transport business in Maraal. When Oza's name was mentioned in front of Ramnaresh's wife, she was shocked.

She thought that Suresh Singh must have blurted out the name after getting a sound beating from the police. At the mention of a third round of blows, she softened a little and divulged that she had received a phone call from Ramnaresh that he was safely ensconced at Madan Oza's farm house.

All the newspapers reported the incident, the day after it happened. It being a police case, Madan Oza advised Ramnaresh to go to Baliya, Ramnaresh's native place. In a day or two he would make the arrangements for Ramnaresh to go to Baliya. But this was not destined to happen. Renuka and her police team had conducted a raid on the farm house. Ramnaresh and his two brothers-in-law tried to escape by the rear exit. Madan Oza was not present at that time. Renuka had nabbed the three of them and presented them before a Magistrate and had them sent to police custody. Ramnaresh's wife was also brought to the court. She was totally confused and was crying. Ramnaresh growled at her.

By that evening, Radha's condition had deteriorated. Jaggu felt miserable and helpless. Parbati had gone back to Maraal. Ramlal was by Jaggu's side. The doctors told them to inform their relatives, if they wished. Jaggu just stared vacuously at the doctors.

In the evening Radha asked the nurse to call Jaggu to her side. She could sense that she was nearing her last hour. Jaggu took her left hand in his. The right one had the saline needle in it. She looked at him with limpid eyes. Although her whole body had become lifeless, her eyes had a sparkle in them.

Jaggu said, "My love, why did you do this to yourself? What made you think that I would no longer accept you? You should not have set yourself on fire."

She replied in a weak voice, "I did not want to live with this impure body. I could not offer it to you."

He said, "This is all nonsense. You have a pure mind, and that is enough for me."

She smiled faintly.

He said, "Did you not think of how I could live without you? Should I commit suicide like you? What will become of me? I have no one but you. I am not able to say anything. (Aami to kichhu bolate parabo na-in Bangala)"

She said, "No. You must continue to face life's challenges. I have one more wish. (na, tumake jibaner sathe zujate hobe. Aar aamaar ek ichha chilo)"

"What is it?" (Bolon toh) said Jaggu.

She said in trembling voice "You must marry again. You will get a new wife. She will bear you a son (Aapni aaro ek baar biye kore neben. Aapni nutan kono stree pete paren. Aapanaake kono din chele hote parabe)."

"Don't say it again. You are not going anywhere. You will survive. I have spoken to the doctor. He has promised to heal you (naa e katha bolabe naa,tumi jabe naa, tumi thakabe, aami doctor sange bolabo, vo tumake thik korabe –In Bangala language) ." Then he began to sob violently. The nurse asked the ward boys to escort him out so as not to disturb the other patients. Jaggu kept telling Radha, "Don't go away, don't go. (tumi jabe na, tumi jabe na)"

Ramlal tried to calm him down. Kali Manjhi also tried to console him.

At four o'clock in the morning, Radha breathed her last. Jaggu had seen her struggle for two hours since 2 o'clock. When she closed her eyes forever, he did not cry. He just gazed at Ramlal. It was as if he had lost his sensitivity. Leaving Kali Manjhi to look after Jaggu, Ramlal went out to make arrangements for the last rites. He looked for a jeep to carry Radha's body to Maral, but it was difficult to get a jeep at such an early hour.

Renuka had instructed the doctors to conduct a postmortem in case of death. As the body could not be handed over in the morning, and it was to be handed over only in the afternoon. Ramlal requested the doctors to conduct the postmortem soon.

Renuka got the news of Radha's death at 7 a.m. She further informed Kirti about it. Kirti decided to go to the hospital. She issued instructions for Radha's cremation and arrangements were under way.

Renuka asked the hospital to hurry up with the postmortem and so there wasn't going to be any delay. Renuka had to change the police record again as Radha had died. She had to present the case before the Magistrate and send Ramnaresh, his wife and his two brothers-in-law to jail. Madan Oza was threatened that he may also be arrested for abetting the criminals. So he was subdued.

Details of the case were being reported in the local newspapers of Ranchi and Ramgadh. It was difficult for Madan Oza to use political pull to put pressure on Renuka. He did try to see if the matter could be settled with money favour. Renuka got the subtle hint through a middleman, but she ignored it. She knew that the Magistrate or the doctor could dilute the case with a monetary compensation. She therefore, maintained a tight grip on the case from the very outset. Madan Oza was unable after trying all means to quash the case.

Radha's body was brought to Maraal. It was first laid to rest in front of Jaggu's hut. Janaki, Parbati and Kali Manjhi's wife had performed some basic rites. It was not possible to bathe the body because of the post mortem. Jaggu just looked at the body in sheer despair. Everyone tried to make him cry. Radha's death was such a terrible shock for him that it engulfed him in vortex of emptiness and silence and there was no life in his eyes. Ramlal took care of the last rites. Radha's brother and sister-in-law arrived from Birbhoom. One could not bear to see their extreme grief and wailing. Jaggu's stony look did not change, he did not cry even meeting his brother in law.

Radha's body was brought to the cremation ground. The Cremation ground was located on the bank of the Damodar river. The pyre was stacked with wooden logs. It was to be lit. A big crowd had gathered. Kirti was also there for the cremation. There were some government workers and some Baniharees. Jaggu was not coming forward to light the pyre. He sat still. Radha's brother held Jaggu's hand and lighted the pyre. As the flames engulfed the body, Jaggu began to sob.

His body began to tremble. Ramlal held him tight. Then Jaggu rested his head on Ramlal's shoulder and gave full vent to his sorrow. He would look at the pyre and scream. All his pent-up emotions from early morning found a release.

The breeze that blew from across the Damodar was not new to Kirti. Even today it played against the strands of her hair. As she looked at the burning pyre, she thought that it was not in anyone's hand to choose where to be cremated. No one could predict where one would have his/her last rites performed. Where was the place of Radha's birth and here was she getting cremated at a faraway place. Did Radha confine her body to the flames happily? Had she lived on, her life would have been a burning pyre. Society would have looked upon her with contempt.

Kirti wondered where would she (herself) be cremated, at which place, Kolkata. Or May be on the bank of the Damodar itself. She didn't know. She didn't even know who would light her pyre.

On the third day after the incident, Kirti had an argument with Mr. Sinha project officer. It was about providing a government ambulance to a non-government worker like Jaggu. It was because of Kirti's intervention that Radha's case had reached the police so quickly. The lady doctor had prepared the case papers based on truth. Most of the officials were in a celebratory mood because of Holi festival. Otherwise they would have put pressure on the Lady Doctor at Maraal to twist the truth. Ramnaresh had the sympathy of people like Prabhunath Singh, Deepak Chatterjee and others and they were very saddened that there was a solid, fool-proof case against Ramnaresh. So all these officials complained about Kirti to Mr. Sinha project officer. Kirti firmly stated that what she had done was on humanitarian grounds; it was a simple, welfare measure.

Sinha said that it was misuse of the government ambulance and Kirti would have to pay the ambulance charges from her pocket.

Kirti said she would pay willingly. Sinha could prepare the bill. But at the same time she demanded that bills be made for all the private trips that officials made in government jeeps.

Sinha hollered at her, "What do you mean?"

Kirti retorted, "I know very well that one day prior to Holi, whose jeeps had been used to get imported whisky bottles from Ramgadh. That is also a gross misuse of government jeeps. Make a bill for that along with the bill for the ambulance."

Sinha stared at her dumb struck.

Kirti quickly left Sinha's office.

... ... Today, while she was sitting in Renuka's house, Kirti recollected all these events.

She herself could not fathom why she had felt so much affection and empathy for Jaggu and Radha; but it had given her a sense of fulfillment in helping them out. Renuka had finished her telephone talk a long time back. But when she came to the drawing room, she saw Kirti lost in her thoughts. Just then Aradhya came calling out to Kirti, "Aunty, aunty," and Kirti came out of her reverie.

Aradhya asked for another chocolate and Kirti promised her that she would get one on her next visit.

Renuka admonished Aradhya and told her not to have too many chocolates.

Aradhya told her that she would take one from Kirti Aunty and not from her.

Kirti and Renuka laughed indulgently.

Aradhya ran into Buaji's arms.

Renuka reminded Kirti that she had been saying something about Jaggu's case, that is, about Radha's husband.

Kirti said "Yes, I was talking of Radha's husband. About Radha, I still shiver in nighttime remembering her face, her body and her tortures."

Ranuka said "In the context of Radha, I feel that though the value of human life is important, there is tendency to neglect it. The crimes against women are on rise. We, the women, who have some status and position should stand united against such crimes. The flow of humanity should be clean and pure like the flow of Ganga river at Gangotri. This flow of humanity should not have been impured by these reckless crimes of rapes, torturs and exploitation of women, by these vulturs of society. They are like the small dirty impure nallahas or tributaries of Ganga making the pure water of humanity dirty, stinky and filthy."

Kirti said that in those days there was a lot of strictness in the mine culture. Therefore, the Impersonation or Baniharee system had been under control. Ramnaresh Yadav, Janu Prasad and others had already lost their jobs. Recently, the Baniharees were rearing their heads up again.

Renuka asked whether Jaggu had become a impersonator (Baniharee) again.

Kirti replied that she did not know. Perhaps he may not have become a impersonator (Baniharee) again. She had not seen him for a long time now. She had not made any enquiries about him.

She further said that the point to be noted was, corruption is an attitude that is deeply entrenched in the minds of Indians. We don't mind paying a bribe just to get a seat or berth on the railway. When we tell the Ticket Collector to adjust a seat, he understands the language. There are similar adjustments in all walks of life.

Renuka said that Kirti could surely understand how strictly she had to adhere to her principles in her career as a police officer. That is why her juniors would ask to be transferred elsewhere or they would get it done secretly. It would be so obvious that they wanted to carry on their corrupt practices unchecked.

Meanwhile Buaji served some snacks (Kachoris) and tea. After partaking of the snacks and tea, Kirti got ready to leave. Renuka asked her driver to drop Kirti at the bus stand.

After Kirti had left, Renuka wondered about Kirti. She knew that Baldev had left her. So she was more worried about Kirti. She felt bad that she could do nothing to alleviate Kirti's loneliness and her desperation. The only thing she could do was to invite Kirti to Ramgadh, let her spend some time with Aradhya and give her a few moments of happiness and lift her spirits a bit.

Renuka surmised that once a person receives a setback in life, there is no bouncing back. It is a decline always and the person loses his sense of right and wrong and has to bear the consequences. The destiny slaps you again and again and you become helpless. Since her college life, Kirti was making the mistakes. If she had on first chance, had agreed for secret abortion without other than family members knowing the pregnancy, she would have had some better chance to get married. She allowed the problem to evaporate and got bad name in society. This had caused a damage to the chance of getting married. On this account also there are double standards in society. If boy does something like this and impregnants girl, his marriage chances are not hampered as compared to girl. The two things they will look for boys, are his income and status of his family. The preference to girls beauty is first and then her education. If something like doubtful character is known she is rejected all through. Renuka thought that kirti continued doing mistake after mistake or the fate forced upon her.

The question why Kirti had been subjected to this misfortune, that thought gnawed Renuka's heart, like a moth struggling to come out of a lotus.

Jaggu fell on bad days again. The Sardarji, Joginder Singh, for whom Jaggu worked, had lost his coal contract. He did not obtain a permit further and more importantly, he got a bigger contract at the Coalfield near Satna in Madhya Pradesh. He was willing to take Jaggu to Satna, but Jaggu did not wish to go that far. He could not bear to leave the hut in which he had lived with Radha.

He still felt her presence beside him, telling him to get up, to fetch water, light the stove, to make tea, take a bath, cook the rice and so on. Each day after getting up, he will be thinking that she is instructing him to do this and that activity. While taking meals, he will feel as if her hand is feeding her. At the end of the day on the bed, he used to imagine as if her hand is stroking though hairs of his head. He had become feeble, physically and emotionally.

Kali Manjhi came up with a proposal. There was an illegal mine at Napanga. It was three kilometers away on the other bank of the river Damodar. Long ago it was an underground mine. The plan was to make it open cast but because of safety issues, the permission had not been granted. It was recognized as an abandoned or unused mine. The old galleries and pillars still existed. When it became difficult to mine the mine and the coal became scarce, the mine was closed down. It remained closed for the past seventeen years. It would be filled with water but after Diwali or in the month of

October most of the water would flow into the Damodar and the water level in the mine would recede. The coal quality was very good. It was like coking coal, 'A'grade. After the coal had been burned, it would turn into soft coke. So this mine had become very well-known. Now, some person called Babulal Mishra was going to run the illegal mine.

Kali Manjhi's situation was similar to Jaggu's situation. He would be troubled by Ramnaresh's men, Naval Prasad and Suresh Singh. So he left Maraal and found a loader's job in Chutkakhana. He had brought this proposal. Besides, they would also be earning more in Napanga. Jaggu had said that he needed more time to think. He was hesitant to pick up a new kind of job.

He thought of consulting Kirti Madam first. He wondered whether she would offer him a job somewhere in Maraal. The last time he had made a mistake and Kirti had scolded him for it. Before she had spoken to Prabhunath Singh and built a background, he had talked to Prabhunath Singh and invited trouble. Ramnaresh had beaten him up for that.

Kali Manjhi was also fed up with life in Maraal, but he was not in any debt. Jaggu felt he was still in debt. He had paid the money lender so much, but the money lender claimed that there was still some balance to be paid. Jaggu never understood the money lender's system of capital and interest. He would take money and deduct it from the interest for two-three months. He never reduced the capital. It was so confusing!

Jaggu went to meet Kirti at her office in the evening. Kirti's clerk was just about to leave. He recognized Jaggu. After Radha's incident, there was hardly anyone in Maraal who did not recognize Jaggu. He informed Kirti and she promptly asked him to come in. The clerk asked her whether he should wait but Kirti told him that he could leave.

Jaggu tried to touch her feet, but Kirti did not let him do it. He muttered, "Pranam, Namaste, (Greetings)" in a servile manner. He stood there until Kirti asked him what had brought him to her office. He said he needed her gracious help. She asked him if he wanted a job. He nodded his head and explained that the Sardarji, who had the loading contract was leaving for Satna and Ramnaresh's men would not let him take up a job anywhere in Maral.

Kirti became thoughtful. She did not know what to say. She said it was difficult to work as casual labour on a government project. Loading Supervisor Ashok Kumar Jha had been suspended, because Jaggu had been caught as a Baniharee. The officials had used all their astuteness to save his job. Three of his increments had been stopped. He had been demoted and transferred to a non-lucrative post in Ichotu area. Prabhunath Singh was very angry with Jaggu.

Jaggu remained silent. Kirti was also immersed in her thoughts.

Then he said, "Can I find work with any contractor?"

She said, "No one will take the risk of hiring you. They think you are a nuisance."

"What should I do, Madam?"

She said, "What can I say? You can go back to your village. You can find work there on the farms."

He thought she had finished speaking and turned to leave. She stopped him.

She asked him, "You have to do all your household chores, don't you? Do you remember Radha often?"

He looked at Kirti. The mention of Radha's name had made him very sad and agitated. "What can I do Madam? I have no choice."

She said, "You can do the same household chores at my bungalow. Stay at my house."

Jaggu looked at Kirti, dumbfounded.

She said, "Don't be afraid. I am not forcing you. Come only if you wish. You don't have to worry about money."

It suddenly dawned on Jaggu that Madam wanted a live-in mate in place of Baldev. He said, "May I ask you something, Madam?"

She asked him to go ahead with his question. He was quiet for a moment. He did not have the courage to ask. She coaxed him to say it.

He said, "After I finish all the work, can I go back to my hut to sleep for the night?" He wanted to tell her that it was Radha's hut and he did not want to leave it.

"No. You can't," Kirti said.

"Must I live like Baldev?" Jaggu asked finally, with courage.

"You have spoken very sensibly. I know you are in debt. I will repay your debt. I will catch hold of that money lender and settle the accounts properly. You don't worry about it. Only...." Said Renuka. She remembered that sentence Baldev had uttered at Ramgadh while arranging for autoriksha. He had suggested that I should find someone to live in with me.

Jaggu became very thoughtful. He did not like this proposal but he did not know how to say it. Finally, he gathered courage and said, "Sarkar, I am a very lowly man. I am fit only to touch your feet and pray to you as a goddess. You have done a lot for me and Radha."

Kirti replied, "Look, you are in need of money and I am in need of a companion; especially of a trustworthy companion like you. You stay with me. Once you move in, you will also want company. I am not asking you to do ----"

She did not complete her sentence. She meant that she is not asking him today itself. That he also understood. He again became thoughtful. He kept quiet. She realized that he is in two minds. He is lured by the money angle. But he does not wish to be enslaved in a different kind of life. The prospect of money did not light up his face. Anyone else in his place would have jumped at the offer. Kirti was convinced that he was just the kind of reliable man she yearned for. She should not let go of him. But how and when could she persuade him?

She asked, "When will you decide?"

He kept quiet.

She said, “Look here. At first you come only during the day to do the household chores. Go to your hut in the evening to sleep. I will pay you Rs 300 per day for now. I don’t pay this much to my maid or cook put together.”

He told her that he would consider the offer and give his reply later. Meanwhile she should also try to get him a job at some contractor’s or builder’s site. He stood with his hands joined in a meek attitude.

She understood his intention and gestured him to leave.

Jaggu Manjhi was in a dilemma. He was unable to come to a decision. He visited Ramlal the next evening in the hope that Ramlal would give him proper advice. Ramlal was not at home. He had gone out with his grand daughter-in-law to her parents’ home. She was pregnant so he was escorting her home for her confinement. Manoj had also not returned from the mine. He was working overtime these days.

Only Janaki and Parbati were at home. Jaggu had turned back from the door as Ramlal wasn’t at home. But Parbati told him to have a cup of tea. Jaggu told her he would have it some other time when Ramlal was at home. But she insisted and said she would have it ready in two minutes. She invited him in. Janaki, mother-in-law of Parbati was sitting in the room. She had heard all the conversation. She disliked Jaggu coming home. She felt that Parbati was taking undue interest in Jaggu. Perhaps something was brewing between them. Since Radha’s death Jaggu’s visits to Ramlal’s house had become more frequent. Parbati also welcomed him warmly, made tea and snacks for him. Jaggu would address Parbati very respectfully as ‘Bhabhi’ (Sister-in-law). He had no inkling about the suspicion in Janaki’s mind.

When Parbati went in to make tea, Janaki asked Jaggu about his work. Jaggu told her the truth that his work with the Sardarji was coming to an end and he was in search of a job.

Janaki suggested that he should go back to his village, Kundapara.

Jaggu told her that his brothers had almost grabbed his land. His brothers had given him his mother's piece of land that was already mortgaged. He had lost it for failure to repay the loan.

Janaki told him that after all one's village was one's own; there was always some way to earn two square meals a day in one's own village. Janaki's other intention was to keep him away also.

Jaggu kept quiet. He could not divulge to Janaki that he still owed the money lender some money. He had been jobless for a while, when Radha died. As he was in a disturbed state of mind and would sometimes report for work and sometimes stay at home. The debt amount got accumulated. The interest he had defaulted had been added to his capital and so his loan amount was huge. The money lender had charged him 10% interest per month. He had then become more systematic in his work afterwards and brought down the debt by half. But half still remained to be repaid.

Parbati was listening to this conversation from the kitchen. She came out with the tea and biscuits. She had learnt how to be a good host when she became the wife of an Executive Engineer.

Parbati told him that recently in her office, she had come across a contractor, an old acquaintance of Shivlal, her husband. He was looking out for people to hire as workers.

"Is he not a contractor with our mine anymore?" Jaggu asked.

Parbati told him that this contractor had got into a problem some time back. One of his workers had made a mistake and a wall had collapsed after that he had not been given any work in the mine at Maraal.

"What is his name?"asked Jaggu.

"I don't know. Someone Babulal...." She said.

"It must be Babulal Mishra," Jaggu surmised.

"I don't know. My husband used to call him Babulal only," Parbati added.

"Is he a good man?" He asked.

"I don't know. My husband never told me about him and I never asked. Yes, but there is one thing..."Parbati stopped mid-sentence.

After a pause, she said, "There is no harm in saying it now. Maaji, Will you be annoyed if I tell Jaggu Bhaiya about it?"

Janaki did not reply.

Parbati says, "This Babulal used to give my husband some money as commission earned from the contract. I know because whenever this man visited us, I used to find some money in my husband's pocket."

Janaki looked embarrassed. She was very angry that her daughter-in-law had told a stranger about her son's corrupt attitude. She went inside in a huff. Parbati understood that Janaki did not like it. She remained quiet and gestured Jaggu that of late Janaki had become very short tempered.

Jaggu got up to leave." Good bye, Bhabhi." He said." Good bye, Aunt (Chachiji)."

But Janaki gave no response. Jaggu went on his way.

On Saturday, Deepak Chatterjee got a phone call in his office. It was from Manas Sengupta, who informed him that Mr. Satish Trivedi had passed away. If possible, Deepak should come to Trivedi's bungalow in the afternoon. The funeral was in the afternoon. Deepak wound up his office work in a hurry. He called up Mr. Sinha, PO to convey the news. Sinha told him that someone from the project must attend the funeral and asked Deepak Chatterjee to attend. He also told him to ensure that the office work was set in order, before he left. It was exactly as Deepak had wished. Before he could even ask for permission to attend the funeral, he had readily been given the instruction to attend. He realized that Sinha Sahib had a good rapport with Trivedi Sahib and so he had made the suggestion to attend. He informed Prabhunath Singh about the death.

Deepak quickly finished his office tasks and after informing the Loading Supervisor, Sumant Singh, he left for Ramgadh.

On arriving at Trivedi's bungalow, Deepak saw only two or three people standing, Headquarters Office worked only half-day on Saturday, so most people had left the office. Forget the whole office; even the Sales Department was absent. Manas informed that the funeral arrangements were almost done.

Deepak asked when was Trivedi's son expected to reach.

Manas said it would take him some time to come from Bangalore. There was no direct flight to Ranchi. He would have to fly via Kolkata or Delhi. He had asked me to go ahead with the rites and not to worry about the money. He was transferring some money into my account.

Just then a truck drew up in front of the house. It belonged to some Civil Contractor attached to Headquarters. Six or seven people were required to lift the bier. Manas made a few phone calls here and there. A few men from sales dept. etc arrived. When the corpse was being put into the truck, The GM, Civil, and the GM, Finance, came out of the adjacent bungalows and stood by the road. Deepak did not understand this attitude towards Mr. Trivedi.

Deepak reached the crematorium in a jeep. There were three people from the Sales Department travelling with him in the jeep. Manas got on to the truck. He was holding the earthen pot used in the rites. There was just one more car coming along. There were four people in the truck, four in the jeep, two in the car and two on the ghat. There were just about twelve people in all at the cremation of a General Manager.

The Ramgadh crematorium was located on the bank of the Damodar river. The funeral pyre was raised at this spot. Everything was done in a haste. Manas had lit the pyre. Once the flames engulfed the body, Manas came and sat next to Deepak. Manas had tears in his eyes. Deepak gently ran his hand over Manas' back to console him and said, "I don't understand—so few people, no relatives, I don't believe this."

Manas told he would explain that later. The truck had driven away. The others returned in the jeep and the car.

At the bungalow these people washed their feet and dispersed. Only Deepak, Manas and the peon from the Sales Department were left behind. The peon sat on a chair outside the bungalow and Deepak and Manas were sitting inside the house. Manas told Deepak that if he wanted to have a bath, he could go home.

Deepak told him that he would rather wait there. Manas opened the refrigerator and pulled out a Coca Cola bottle.

He fetched two glasses and poured the drink into it. He took one for himself and offered one to Deepak. Deepak reminded him about the peon outside. Manas told him that he would tell the peon to have a drink of Coca Cola later because it was the peon who would be locking the bungalow and keeping the keys. "Do not bother about him, I am paying him always". Manas told Deepak.

Both of them sipped their coke. Placing his half-empty glass on the tea- table, Manas remarked that one chapter had come to an end. He had borne this responsibility for a very long time and was now free from it.

Deepak said, "I appreciate your good deed, but...."

Manas said, "I know what that 'but' implies. You are curious to know about the situation here. I will give you some important information. I was going to tell you at the hospital that day, but could not."

"What is it?" Deepak asked.

"Trivedi Sahib was suffering from AIDS." Informed Manas.

"Oh! My God!"

Manas told him the details. "It all started eight or nine months ago. But there is a background leading to it. Trivedi was not an honest man. He was corrupt like you and myself. But there is a system or formula about how much of the black money should be saved, how much should be spent and on what items to be spent. Sometimes we make so much money that we tend to splurge. You know very well that Trivedi was a womanizer. His wife knew about his philandering ways and also that he was making a lot of dirty money. "

"He had links with the coal mafia. Besides He would send money directly to the MD, so he had the MD's patronage. Trivedi would love to go to Kolkata for his flings. I am not sure, but I think Madan Oza was helping him in this habit. Today that same Madan Oza didn't even bother to attend the funeral. Trivedi had called him up once or twice from the hospital. Now Madan Oza is playing to the tunes of Uttam Singh, the new GM. Madan Oza is that kind of a man. Anyway, let him be."

"I think Trivedi caught this disease in the whore houses of Sonagachhi in Kolkata. He realized it rather late. Bhabhiji had also contacted it from him. She had gone to Bangalore to help her daughter-in-law in her pregnancy. There She had some health problem so her son sent her for a check-up and she was detected with AIDS. The son who lives in America and the one in Banagalore had come here and given a piece of their mind to their father. They had told their father that they would not even touch his dead body. Trivedi had confided all this to me while he was in the hospital. The son had asked for my bank details and mentioned that since I am retired I should not face a financial burden. They were grateful to me for doing this humanitarian deed. They said that they could never forget that their father had in a way, killed their mother. Their father had started his own treatment but never thought about treating his wife, who had caught the disease from him. Do you know what this son said to me? He said, "My father is not a human being, he is a beast."

"I did my part. On the basis of the relationship I had with Trivedi Sahib, I did what my conscience told me. He had saved me from a vigilance case. Perhaps we were related in our previous births. I don't know."

"You see, Trivedi's ignomity as a womanizer, his AIDS affliction had spread like wild fire amongst the relatives and so no one bothered to attend the funeral. His own son did not come, how can you expect other relatives to attend? It is the same in the office lately. Since GM Uttamsingh is on tour he did not attend."

"What about the immersion of the ashes, the thirteenth day ritual, the Shraddh (Mourning ritual after death)?" Deepak asked.

Manas replied that he was going to perform all the rites. Shraddh and thirteenth day rite would just be observed as a formality. The son from America has said that a donation in his father's name should be made to some old age home in Ranchi. He would remit the money soon.

Deepak was bewildered. He was surprised at the sons' behaviour. One was in America but at least the other was in India. He thought about how corruption could result in complete downfall. One had to suffer the evil consequences not just in one's life but even after death!

He remembered to have read somewhere, that the good or bad deeds/actions "Karma" not only of this birth but also of previous birth affect the destiny of the person. Only few persons are lucky maintaining good health without any family problem, even after doing so much corruption, may be on the basis of some good "Karma" in this birth and previous birth. Whereas, in general, persons like Trivedi have to suffer like anything.

On Kali Manjhi's insistence, Jaggu agreed to work in the illegal mine at Napanga. There were total eight workers only.. There was a ditch near the mine. The flow of water seemed to be blocked, one had to wade through knee-deep water, and then take a pathway up to the mine. Someone had tried to enter it earlier and that is why there was a big hole in the wall. This spot was located beneath a hillock and at the end of it, there was a flat area like a valley. The eight workers widened the hole and entered the pit. There was a steep slope inside towards the gallery from where the mine extended deep. There were pillars everywhere. One corner, or one phase in mining jargon had been found. It was low in height and there was very little water.

There was a clever chap called Bala Munda among the workers. He had worked in an underground mine before. But once when he was drunk, he had burnt an electric motor by mistake, so he was dismissed. He was experienced so he had brought along a mosquito spray pipe and sprayed some pesticide before entering the mine, to kill the various insects. Then he lit a torch to ensure that there were no snakes or reptiles inside. He managed to get mining lamps from somewhere and there were 24 sets of lamps. He would manage the battery charging later. He first tried to raise the roof of the mine so that work could be done easily. There were two small battery-operated drilling machines. The roof was drilled and filled with explosives and blown to make the coal fall. The coal had to be collected in baskets and transported to the other side of the ditch by walking through knee deep water. To keep the coal heaps hidden from public eye, stone and mud piles had to be made around them. In the evening, when it became dark, a truck would arrive and carry the coal away.

Even if a little coal was collected in two or three days, the half-filled truck would take it away during initial days. After a few days, at least a truck load of coal would be collected on at least alternate day, finding that this was a safe place for keeping the coal. The truck would take the coal once in two or three days.

At the time of exploding the gun powder, everyone except Bala Munda went away to the other side of the ditch. One of Bala's helpers had been trained by Bala Munda. Both together would carry on the work efficiently. The daily wage decided was Rs 400 plus some more if a large quantity of coal was mined. Babulal Mishra, who had hired them, would come once in two or three days and check the progress of the work. Once in his conversation with Bala, he used the term, 'Big Master/Big Boss'. The truck belonged to the Big Boss. Jaggu and Kali Manjhi asked Bala Munda the name and address of the Big Boss but Bala had said that he did not know. Babulal would pay them weekly wages.

Since Napanga was termed as an 'Abandoned mine', RCL had not provided any security. Illegal mining was prohibited by Law. This did not stop Babulal from venturing deep into the mine with a minimum work force.

Two months had passed in this manner. Jaggu Manjhi was very happy to earn so much money. He was paid extra money of rupees three thousand as bonus also. He conveyed his happiness to Ramlal. Ramlal cautioned him to be careful. Ramlal insisted that he should continue the search for ulternate jobs also.

Jaggu took Kali Manjhi along to meet the money lender. He asked the money lender several penetrating questions about his payments. Earlier the money lender was not keen on having the loan repaid; it was more profitable to collect interest on pending loans. But because of Jaggu's irregular income, he was now interested in getting back the capital. He conveyed this to Jaggu, that the loan repayment is nearing completion. He had already earned ten times of the money inintially loaned to Jaggu.

At 10 p.m. on one Saturday night, Kali Manjhi's wife came to Ramlal's house. Ramlal was asleep at the time. Her arrival at such a late hour made him anxious. She told him that Kali Manjhi had not returned home. He usually returned by 7 or 8 o'clock in the evening. She had looked for him everywhere, even at the wayside liquor dens. She had enquired at all his friends' houses. Her mother-in-law and her son were also with her.

"Have you checked with Jaggu ?" Ramlal asked.

"Even Jaggu Bhaiya has not returned. His hut is locked." She told.

Ramlal got worried that both Jaggu and Kali had not returned. But it was difficult to look for them in the darkness. He told Kali Manjhi's wife that they might return in the morning; perhaps they had additional work to do and had been provided with dinner at the mining site and decided to sleep there for the night. He somehow managed to convince her to go back home and inform him if they did not return in the morning. He would go and look for them. Although he had sent her away for the time being, he himself could not sleep. The fact that Jaggu Manjhi had not returned, made him feel very uneasy and he had all sorts of wayward thoughts. Ramlal rose at 5.30 in the morning and finished his ablutions. Janaki was worried too. She saw that her husband had become very restless and pensive on hearing about Jaggu. She too got up early and made him some tea. She gave him tea and biscuits. Ramlal said to Janaki, "When Manoj wakes up, ask him to get ready quickly. I want to take him along with me."

Ramlal left his house and went to Jaggu's hut first. The hut was still locked. He then woke up Narsa Munda (Baniharee of Ayodhya Prasad). As it was a Sunday, everyone was having a relaxed schedule. Together, they walked towards Kali Manjhi's house. They met Kali Manjhi's wife who was already on her way to Ramlal's house. The expression on her face told Ramlal that Kali had not returned. Then Ramlal and Narsa collected two more men to go along with them. Manoj also came looking for his grandpa.

This team of five made their way to Napanga. Kali Manjhi's wife also wanted to go, but they stopped her. She then started crying and told everyone that Kali and Jaggu had disappeared.

As the team came near Napanga, they found two bicycles lying on the road. This indicated that two men had entered the mine but had not come out. There was a ditch along the path to Napanga. From this side of the ditch, one could not see across the other side. The mine or existence of any person was not visible. They decided to wade through the ditch. Manoj told his grandfather not to walk through so much water as he suffered from asthma and the cold water would aggravate it. But Ramlal was adamant. He crossed the ditch with them. Then they found out the footpath leading up to the mine. They could see footprints of shoes and chappals on the path. They reached the mine. Manoj had brought two torches.

From that point they called out loudly, "Jaggu!Kali !" There was no response. Narsa asked Ramlal and Manoj to wait outside while he and two others made their way to inside. Ramlal asked him to be careful. They had just about reached a slope, when they saw that the roof of the mine had collapsed and the mine was closed. It was a very big roof fall. There was no way to know whether there was a proper sand stowing or not. But in all these years the stowed sand might have been washed away. That was the reason, coal could be obtained. A piece of the pillar had also fallen outside. This was a proof that a roof had fallen and the workers were buried under that roof. Or maybe they were alive but trapped under it. Narsa and his companions tried banging with sticks, but the huge boulders of coal did not budge. They came out and informed Ramlal about the situation. Ramlal began to cry. Manoj consoled him. Ramlal said they must go back and inform the police.

By now the news had spread in the shanty colony of the workers that Jaggu and Kali Manjhi have vanished. Everyone was especially worried to hear about Jaggu's name. Parbati wanted to inform Kirti Madam, whom she would meet in the office every day. She asked her mother-in-law whether she should do it. Her mother-in-law snapped at her, "Do it if you want to." Parbati did not understand why her mother-in-law got so upset with her at the mention of Jaggu's name. Parbati went over to Kirti's bungalow and informed her about Kali and Jaggu and about the fact that Ramlal and Manoj had gone to Napanga.

After Parbati left, Kirti became pensive. Just then she received a call from Renuka. Renuka asked her that since it was a Sunday, would she like to come over and meet Aradhya. Kirti replied that she would give it a thought. Renuka sensed the worry in her voice and asked if there was a problem. Kirti told her that indeed there was a problem— Jaggu Manjhi had vanished.

Renuka asked,"Radha Manjhi's husband, you mean?"

Kirti said, "Yes."

The Police Officer in Renuka is suddenly alerted. "Give me the details."

Kirti told her that she did not know the details. "There is an abandoned mine at Napanga, that is, an old mine that is not in use anymore. It seems these people had gone there to do illegal mining. There might have been an accident there. Four or five people have gone in search of them. I will let you know when they return."

Renuka said, "I will wait for your call. Be sure to call."

Renuka put down the receiver but her sixth sense told her that something was wrong. She again called up Kirti and asked her whether Jaggu alone had disappeared or there were others like him. Kirti told her that Jaggu's companion Kali Manjhi was also missing.

"Oh, I see."

"Have you informed the Maraal Police station?" Kirti asked.

"No, not yet. Have you any idea of how many people might be there in the illegal mine? Surely not twenty or twenty – five? If so many have gone missing I have to inform all the other Police Stations accordingly. Maraal and others nearby" said Renuka.

"I do not know for sure. I think it must be a very small team of workers—may be eight or ten workers; or ten to fifteen at the most." Kirti said.

"Even if it is eight or ten, it's a terrible thing that they should all meet with an accident or die in one stroke." Said Renuka.

Kirti said, "I forgot to mention to you that Jaggu had come to me. He had lost his transport job and requested me to put him on a job."

Renuka said, "You should have put him on some other job."

Kirti told, "Because of Radha's case, no one was willing to take him on a job."

Renuka said, "I will inform the police station. But you must gather information about the men who have gone into the mine and let me know."

Kirti assured her that she would do the needful.

When Renuka called up the Maraal police station, the Inspector on duty was not present. Renuka told the constable about the incident at the mine and told him to gather some more information about the workers. She also told him to get the inspector to talk to her.

By then Ramlal and his companions had reached the police station. The inspector was also present. He made a written report. He decided to visit the spot and then take action accordingly. He wrote an approximate figure of ten men missing. He took out his jeep to go to the spot. Narsa Munda and Manoj went with him to show the spot. Manoj told his grandfather to go home and not get wet again with the water in the ditch. The inspector rang up Renuka to inform her that he was visiting the spot.

Ramlal went home and changed his clothes. Parbati told him that she had already informed Kirti Madam. Ramlal said he too would go and meet Kirti Madam. Janaki told him to have some breakfast first. She was concerned that Ramlal had got drenched and walked back all the way. Ramlal sat down to have breakfast respecting his wife's concern.

Ramlal said he did not know for which contractor Jaggu and Kali worked. He did not know who their Master was. They had never told him his name. Or maybe they had but he had forgotten due to old age. The moment he said this, Parbati told him that perhaps Jaggu's master's name was Babulal Mishra. She told him that once when he had gone to drop their grand daughter-in-law at her parents' place, Jaggu Manjhi had come home and mentioned the name. She had also told Jaggu that when her husband was alive, this Mishra used to take up contracts in Maraal. Ramlal was grateful that she knew the name.

Ramlal then went to meet Kirti. He met Suresh Singh on the way. Suresh Singh asked him if there was something wrong.

Ramlal did not want to tell him. So he just said that nothing was wrong. Suresh Singh was sure that there was certainly something wrong.

On meeting Kirti, Ramlal narrated the whole incident. He mentioned the name of Babulal Mishra. Kirti kept him seated and conveyed all the information to Renuka. She asked Renuka if she had any questions for Ramlal. Renuka told her to hand over the phone to Ramlal.

Ramlal held the phone and said, "Hello, Madam Sahiba, Madam Sahiba."

Renuka asked, "I want to ask you whether the fallen roof was the last roof or did the mine extend beyond that?"

Ramlal said, "I don't understand. Whether there was roof ahead or not. How does it matter?"

Renuka said, "If it is not the last roof, then perhaps Jaggu is alive and he and the others cannot walk out of the mine."

Now Ramlal understood it in a flash. He said, "Yes, Madam Sahiba, it is possible that this is not the last roof. Jaggu might be alive." The old man's voice trembled as he said this and he quickly handed over the phone to Kirti.

Renuka told Kirti, "First give me Sinha Sahib's number. I will talk to him. Your mine rescue team will be able to work more efficiently than our police team. I will call you again. Meanwhile, keep handy the phone numbers of the Security In-Charge and the mines Safety Officer of Ichotu area. I have the phone number of the Area GM. I will talk to him just now.

Kirti said she would have the phone numbers ready.

Renuka, "And I need you to do one more thing. Get some information about Babulal Mishra, where he lives, the names of his colleagues or partners, if he has any, does he work alone, or whether he has a boss and so on."

Kirti told her that everything would be done.

Renuka then informed all the police stations to enquire about the missing persons. She requested Mr. Sinha to send the rescue team and liaise with the Inspector at Maraal. She told him that she was going to speak with their GM, Ichotu area too. She requested him once again to have the rescue team ready. She had once saved Sinha from being beaten up by the union workers and so he promptly agreed to do whatever she said.

She apologized to the Area GM for disturbing him on a Sunday, but the matter was serious enough to seek his help. He promised to help her by all means and also instruct the Security Officer and the Mine Safety Officer to extend whatever help they could.

Renuka requested the Mine Safety officer of Area office to get some more rescue teams from other mines. It would be great if they could save the lives of the poor workers. She then requested the Area Security Officer to depute his security guards along with her police team. There would be a crowd of onlookers at the accident site and they would need to be controlled. She herself would be away in pursuit of the culprits.

The Security Officer promised her that he himself would be present at the site and she need not worry. He too needed police help several times, so he thought it best to cooperate.

Rescue teams were in readiness everywhere. Ambulances also got their stand-by orders.

The Inspector from Maraal Police Station returned from the spot. He reported to Renuka that he did not understand the mine interior, but he had seen the fallen roof. It would take several experienced men to clear the debris. It was uncertain how many men were trapped under the debris, but a cowherd said he had seen seven or eight people working at the site.

They would dump the coal on the other bank of the ditch and once in two or three days, a truck would come in the evening and take it away.

Renuka ordered him to have the police team ready and to cooperate with the mining team that would be on its way. She could not come because she was looking for the culprits. She told him that other teams from other police stations would also join them. She also asked whether he had any idea of who the perpetrator of the crime was but he said that he had no idea.

Kirti found out that Babulal belonged to Ichotu and operated his business from there. He moved around on a motorcycle. She promptly gave this information to Renuka. Renuka ordered the police station at Ichotu to hunt for Babulal and arrest him and send him to Ramgadh.

Renuka received reports of missing men from other police stations too. She estimated that there were eight men missing. She again called up the GM, Ichotu Area to depute a responsible senior officer to take charge of the rescue operation. Even if she stood there, she would not be able to control it well. The GM said that he would depute the Area Safety Officer. She requested him to send teams from all the various other mines. The Inspector from Maraal would guide them to the spot. Then Renuka reported the incident to the IG (Inspector General) at Ranchi, Capital of Jharkhand state. IG issued orders for the culprits to be arrested immediately. He conjectured that a big name or perhaps the coal mafia was involved.

Renuka wondered if coal mafia could mean Madan Oza. Oza was playing hide and seek with the police for a long time. He had to be nabbed. She sent her informers out to look for Madan Oza.

Four rescue teams reached Napanga. The Area Security Officer and the Safety Officer were also there. One police team entered the mine and the others waited on the other bank of the ditch. The Rescue operation was working under the supervision of the Area Safety Officer. He realized that the darkness made the work difficult. Only manual work would take a long time.

So he called for a generator set in truck and laid cables in the mine to create enough bright light in the deep mine. He also put up two small fans. Two drill machines were carefully breaking the coal boulders. They were on the constant look for any sign of the missing men. A crowd was gathering on the other side of the ditch. They were prohibited from crossing the ditch. There were newspaper reporters in the crowd. They too had been stopped from coming forward.

Suresh Singh had sensed that something was amiss when he had come across Ramlal in the morning. He had met Naval Prasad and they went around Maral. They learned that Jaggu and Kali had gone missing. They were delighted to hear it. They were eager to convey this good news to Madan Oza. In their excitement they rang up Madan Oza and told him the good news that Jaggu was no more and perhaps his friend Kali Manjhi was dead as well.

Madan Oza did not sound happy. He sounded very worried. He asked cautiously when the incident happened. Naval Prasad declared happily that we wanted to finish off Jaggu, but now his life that has come to an end.

Madan Oza shouted into the phone, "When did you get this news?"

Naval Prasad came to his senses and said, "We came to know this morning. It seems they had gone to Napanga Abandoned Mine yesterday."

Madan Oza putdown the phone. The truck had not gone to collect coal the previous evening, so he had no knowledge about the incident.

Naval Prasad wondered what was wrong with his boss that day. The boss had not complimented him for the good news.

Renuka received some positive news from Ichotu that Babulal had been arrested. He was trying to escape on his motorcycle when he was apprehended. He was being brought to Ramgadh.

Renuka wished to go to Napanga and oversee the rescue work. She felt restless. She mentioned this to Kripal Singh who told her that she had given adequate mining instructions and there was no need for her to go personally. He admired her knowledge about mining. She replied modestly that she had once seen a similar mining accident case in the past and could therefore talk so much about it. Then she told him about her talk with the IG and how he had mentioned the Coal Mafia hand in it. She also mentioned her doubts about Madan Oza.

Kripal Singh told her not to worry as he was there by her side as her husband and Collector of the District. (mai hoo Naa—In hindi language)

Kripal Singh now got into action. He made a few phone calls and confirmed to Renuka that Madan Oza was indeed involved. Once Babulal was brought to Ramgadh, she would be sure. Then he told Renuka to put road blocks along Dhanbad Road, Barkakana Road and Rajrappa Road (all roads passing through Ramgadh); and to have the police check all vehicles and to send out policemen in civil clothes to the Ramgadh bus stand and railway station.

Renuka thanked Kripal Singh for his whole-hearted cooperation with valuable suggestions .

He smiled and held her hand and pressed it gently and said "Dear, I know you will be successful in this mission of arresting the main culprit, who is responsible for genocide of innocent labours."

Renuka said "Hope so"

Krupal said "You have organized this total operation brilliantly and immaculately for both mine rescue operation and culprit identification. I doubt myself, whether I could have acted so fast."

Renuka told "You are not only my lifepartner but also benovelence partner for the people of whole Ramgadh district people"

Until then Renuka had been handling the whole affair from home. But now she felt she must go to the Police Control Room to implement the road blockades (Nakabandi) and other methods. Kripal Singh gave his consent and asked her to call him again.

Babulal Mishra was taken to the interrogation room immediately on reaching Ramgadh. Renuka was present in the room. During the interrogation he said that he was running the mine himself, he did not have any Master or Boss. Renuka asked him to name the owner of the truck that transported the coal. She knew he did not possess any truck. She had gone through the truck owners' record at the RTO. She gave him two blows on his hand with her stick. He writhed in pain and agreed to tell the whole story.

Renuka told the constable to give him some water, and the water was splashed on his face. Only a few drops fell into his mouth. He asked for more water to drink. She asked him whether Madan Oza was his boss. He admitted it with a nod of his head. She then let him have a glass of water. Then she told the police to record his confession statement and get his signature upon it. She realized that it was important to take Madan Oza into custody.

With so many rescue teams there was rapid progress in the rescue operation. It was a massive roof fall. The pillars had broken. Two galleries had collapsed. Perhaps the blasting done on the previous day had disturbed the layers of coal. Despite the enormity of the task, the rescue work was going on smoothly. A first dead body was found within the first two hours. Seven or eight people were called to identify the body. Ramlal wanted to cross the ditch once more to identify the body. Kali Manjhi's wife also wanted to go in. But Narsa Munda went ahead of Kali's wife and Ramlal after detaining them. He brought the news that the dead person was someone from Gola town. The dead body was wrapped in a sheet and a post mortem would be conducted as per the rule. The body would be handed over to the relatives only after the post mortem. This was police work. A loud wailing could be heard as it became obvious that there was very little chance of finding any survivors.

Kirti tried to ring up Renuka but there was no response. Renuka too was busy in the police Control room. Kirti was restless and agitated. She felt that on that day she should have compelled Jaggu to come and live with her in the bungalow. He was in need of money but he could not forget Radha either. Jaggu and Radha loved each other ardently. She felt that this intensity may forever dissipate into space today, god knows. She thought that value of human life is important, but the greedy and powerful persons make the other humans to suffer. Sometimes, the human life is treated less than life of animal like horse or cow or dog, though usefull. The humanity suffers a lot and the poor and helpless people like Radha and Jaggu have to sacrifice.

She felt so restless that she called her driver on overtime duty on Sunday and asked him to drive her to Napanga.

Renuka was infuriated and excited to know that Madan Oza was the owner of Napanga mine. She had informed Kripal Singh about it. Then she sent a police team to Oza's Depot and Farmhouse. But there was no sign of Madan anywhere. As Kripal Singh had instructed her, she had posted men at the bus stand and at the railway station. As an additional precaution, she had posted some men in civil clothes at the Barkakana Railway Junction. Barakakana is a major station connecting so many Big cities like Delhi, Kolkata, Ranchi, Patna etc. She got her first break-through from Barkakana at 4 o'clock in the evening. She got the information from her team at Barkakana that with the assistance of the Railway Police, they were able to nab Madan Oza.

But the man they had caught said that he is not Madan Oza. He shows us the Driving License with the name Krishnapal Singh on it.

"I hope you have caught the real Madan Oza, and not someone else?" Renuka enquired.

The policeman from Barkakana reported, "Yes Madam. We can recognize him. But today he has shaved off his huge moustache and shaved his head and gone bald. Instead of his usual Dhoti-Kurta, he is dressed in trousers and shirt. He claims he is not Madan Oza and begs to be allowed to go to Patna."

Renuka told him, "If you are certain that he is Madan Oza, put him in handcuffs. I will send a police van from here. Until then, hold him in the Railway Police cabin. Do not let him go to the Lavatory or anywhere. When the van arrives, put him in it and bring him here."

From her office, Renuka telephoned husband, Kripal Singh to give him the news. He said, "Congratulations, Madam. You took such quick action early in the morning so you were able to lay your hands on the pawn. It would have taken three-four months to find him in Patna."

She said, "Thank you Sir, for your cooperation and suggestions."

Kripal Singh laughed slightly over the telephone.

There was a lot of wailing at Napanga. The women folk looked crestfallen. They wept hysterically. It was difficult to control them. The crowd of onlookers was getting bigger. The security guards and the police were having a tough time controlling them every second. Everyone was trying to cross the ditch and go into the mine. They were being cordoned off. A coal mine truck was washed and requisitioned to carry the dead bodies. Two doctors attached to the Mines were also present. With great difficulty, they were sent into the mine.

One could not bear to see the lamentation of Kali Manjhi's wife. There were seven people who could identify the bodies, sent on the mine side of ditch. Every time a body was identified by someone, he was escorted to the other side of the ditch.

Due to a massive roof fall, a large amount of coal had to be cleared. With the help of some labourers, the coal was being brought out and thrown into the ditch. This had become necessary in order to clear the place of coal blocks. Only five bodies were found until then.

Three of them were from Gola, and two from Topa town. Bala Munda and his partner were from Topa. Only body of partner of Bala Munda was found. Then Jaggu's body was found as the sixth one. Narsa recognized the body. His eyes were filled up with tears. He wanted to come out and tell Ramlal but had to wait inside to identify Kali Manjhi's body. The Security officer from Maraal sent one of his men across the ditch to give the sad news to Ramlal. He said he should break the news gently to Kirti Madam and not shout. Kirti Madam would convey it to others. As soon as the man crossed the ditch, everyone looked at him anxiously. He quietly walked towards Kirti and told her the news in a soft tone. Kirti screamed, "Jaggu is no more." Ramlal was standing next to her. He again asked Kirti in disbelief. She told him that it is true that Jaggu was no more. Ramlal began to cry and started thumping on to the ground. The slight hope he had, was dashed to ground. Manoj also could not stop his tears. He sat down to comfort his grandfather. Kirti also went towards Ramlal and tried to comfort him.

The police standing near the ditch sent a wireless message to Renuka about the six dead bodies, including that of Jaggu.

Wife of Kali Manjhi's lamentations had reached a crescendo. Her mother in law also started crying too much, with likely news of her son's death. Jaggu Manjhi's death had dashed the last bit of hope she had about Kali's survival. Most of the people from Gola and Topa had gone back to give the news to the people in their respective towns. Some women had come to Napanga, others were still in their towns.

Finally, Narsa Munda had to identify Kali Manjhi's body. He was overwhelmed with grief but had to control himself. He did not wait there for a second after identification. The moment he crossed the ditch, the people surrounded him. Kali Manjhi's wife looked at him with questioning eyes. He pointed towards the sky indicating that he had gone to heaven. She gave a heart-wrenching wail. Narsa Munda hugged Ramlal and wept. He muttered that he had lost both his companions. It became difficult to console Kali Manjhi's distraught mother. She had started banging her head on the earth in anguish.

The last body to be recovered was that of Bala Munda. There was still some life left in him. Both his legs had been crushed under the weight of coal. A water bottle was found near his body. Perhaps he had just come in to sip water or just had a sip when the roof collapsed.

The doctors quickly administered oxygen. They had come prepared with saline, injections and other equipments which were kept in the ambulance. Four men quickly picked up Bala Munda and put him in the ambulance. There was a chance that he could be saved. His legs would have to be amputated. He would stay alive in that handicapped state, a living witness to the incident, for the court and the world at large.

The rescue operation came to an end in this manner. It was more of a corpse finding operation than a rescue operation. Every time a body was found and identified, Renuka would be told on the walkie-talkie. With every death, Renuka's anger towards Madan Oza mounted. One by one the bodies were loaded into the truck. The truck was surrounded by people. Kali Manjhi's wife yelled in front of the truck that she wanted to see her husband. With her, there were two more women who had just been widowed, one from Gola and one from Topa, The police allowed the three widows to get on to the truck and see their husbands. Their lamentations pierced the sky. Kirti departed from the scene. Renuka had been trying to call her on the phone, but she had not noticed them.

Renuka had instituted an identification parade for Madan Oza. Although he had disguised himself skillfully, the Ramgadh police were familiar with his face. There were times when these police constables had received gifts from him on the occasion of Diwali and Holi festivals. Now the circumstances had changed. One of the policemen told Renuka that Madan had wiped off the vermilion on his forehead, and removed the golden rings on his fingers. But he still had the familiar thick and long gold chain around his neck. There was a small locket on the chain. He had hidden the chain under his shirt. The police had pulled it out from under his collar. His face turned white when we pulled his chain. He stopped chanting "My name is Krishnapal Singh, Krishnapal Singh." At Ramgadh Police Station, when his suitcase was searched through, the policemen found a lot of items——Eighteen lakh rupees in cash, 10 gold wrist bands, 15 golden finger rings, 08 pass books, check books and nameless property registration papers. They were kept under his usual clothes—dhoti, kurta and jacket. The police had enough incriminating evidence for the court case. Renuka bashed him up with baton so many times, accusing him for killing so many people.

On the next day in the evening, the last rites of Jaggu and Kali Manjhi were performed jointly at the Maraal crematorium. There was a deathly silence in Maraal colony and the hutments. Many government labourers, impersonators (Baniharee) labourers and coal loaders were present at the cremation. The ladies in the neighbourhood had come to comfort and console Kali Manjhi's mother and wife. Parbati and Janaki were deeply grieved and wept inconsolably.

On the banks of the Damodar, at the spot where Radha's body had been confined to the flames, Jaggu also found his last resting place. As the flames rose from his burning pyre in the sky, it was as if he was saying, "Radha, Wait, I am coming with you, don't go alone (Aami tumar sange aajbo, thak, tumi eka jabe naa –in Bangala language)." Ramlal lit the pyre. He thought that he had already lost his real son and now he had lost his adopted son and was lighting his pyre.

Kirti too was there, standing still and silent. It occurred to her again and again that one day she too would be confined to the flames on the banks of the Damodar, but who will light her pyre?